"Misty, what are you running from?"

His directness caught me off guard.

"Why do you ask that?" I tried to sound casual, but his penetrating gaze assured me he wasn't fooled. Should I tell him? I ached to talk about Dave, to pour out my heartache to someone, to hear words of sympathy. I guess what I really wanted was for someone to tell me how to get Dave back. Glenn was a man. He could tell me what to do from a man's point of view. But did I dare expose my heart to a near stranger?

I took a deep breath and spoke softly. "Maybe I *am* running."

"You can tell me about it—if you want to."

I wanted to. I told him the whole sad story—from being in love and practically engaged to Dave, down to the telephone conversation with Sharon and my escape from Reno.

"Then you gave up your job so you wouldn't have to face Dave?"

"Of course! How could I stand to see him, knowing he didn't love me any more?"

"But from what you've told me, you have done nothing to be ashamed of—so why should you run? If you had it to do again, it would have been best to talk it over."

"But there was nothing to talk over! Dave wanted me to—to—" I bit my lower lip. "And Sharon was there—ready and willing."

"Misty—" Glenn's voice was gentle. "Misty, you can't fault a man for being a man. Without God's help, one's baser instincts often take over. . . . Your Dave is no worse than many men."

My mouth dropped open and I felt a hot flush of anger. "Then I don't want him . . . or *any other man!*"

IN
COMES
LOVE

Mab Graff Hoover

Serenade
BOOKS

of the Zondervan Publishing House
Grand Rapids, Michigan

IN COMES LOVE
Copyright © 1983 by The Zondervan Corporation,
1415 Lake Drive, S.E.,
Grand Rapids, Michigan 49506

Library of Congress Cataloging in Publication Data

Hoover, Mab Graff.
   In comes love.

   I. Title.
PS3558.06333I6   1983   813'.54   83-6691
ISBN 0-310-50022-2

Edited by Anne Severance
Designed by Kim Koning

Printed in the United States of America

85 86 87 88 89 / 8 7 6 5 4 3 2

To my husband, Joe, who taught me all I know
about romance.

CHAPTER 1

THE YELLOW CAMARO REELED wildly across two right lanes, then left the highway with tires screaming and a bone-jarring crunch. The steering wheel felt like an angry snake in my hands as I struggled to keep the little car from turning over. When I finally got it stopped, I fell back against the seat and let out my breath in a moan. I turned off the ignition and for a moment I just sat there, staring out at the sandy shoulder, weeds, and beyond the headlights—thick darkness. I leaned forward and rested my head on the steering wheel. As I relived my brush with death, I began to shake uncontrollably.

Night driving wasn't one of my best accomplishments, partly because I hadn't done much of it, and partly because I wouldn't wear my glasses. These facts, coupled with a broken heart, had almost been fatal. I knew I was driving too fast when I left Reno, but I didn't care! I had to get away. I must have been doing seventy-five when the back of a semi-truck loomed up in the headlights. For a moment I froze, then at the last possible moment I stood on the brakes and yanked the wheel with all my strength, just missing the eighteen-wheeler by a few feet.

"Maybe it would have been just as well," I whimpered there in the dark, hugging myself in an effort to quit shaking. At least the struggle would be over. Life without Dave wasn't worth living. A lump formed in my throat, and I put my fist to my lips. I would not cry anymore! I had cried almost constantly since the telephone conversation. Dave—my Dave—loved another woman.

He and I had been going together since my last year at the University, and almost from the first week we had talked about marriage. It was settled, at least in my mind, that we would get married as soon as Dave got his master's degree. He had even given me a promise ring—a delicate, golden circle with a tiny diamond. "Sugar," he had said when he slipped it on my finger, "we have to wait awhile, but this should give you a clue to my feelings."

In the dark I rubbed the empty place on my finger and began to sob. I had loved that ring. But when I left the apartment tonight, I had folded the golden circle in a tissue, addressed an envelope to Dave, and dropped it in the mail. Now, with an actual pain in my heart, I wondered if *she* would wear it. The memory of her sultry voice on the phone tormented me. If only I hadn't called!

As a rule I never called Dave unless there was an emergency. Tonight there had been one when the mechanic at the service station couldn't finish my car before six o'clock. "Sure sorry it's taking so long," he had called to me as he ran to pump gas for another customer. "My boss got sick this afternoon and I'm running the station alone."

"That's okay," I said, but I stewed inside. He had never taken this long before to service the car. I looked at my watch and sighed. "May I use the phone?" I asked when he

8

came back to the grease rack. "I've got a dinner date at six and it's already five-thirty."

"You bet!" he answered. "Phone's in the office—and tell him I'll have you out of here by six for sure!"

Dave would probably be dressed and ready to go out the door, I thought, as I dialed his number. I hoped he'd remember to wear something he could work in. Our plan was to eat dinner, then go back to the apartment, pack all my stuff, and load it in the car. Then in the morning I would drive across town and move in with a girl friend so I could be close to a temporary job I had landed.

When a woman answered Dave's phone, I couldn't speak. Did I have the wrong number? At last, stupidly, I said, "Dave?"

She giggled. "Nope! It's not Dave!"

"Who is this?" I blurted, forgetting my manners.

"It's Sharon." Her voice implied that I should have known. "Dave's girl, Sharon."

Sharon? Had Dave ever mentioned a Sharon?

"Dave won't be back until about ten," she volunteered. "Do you want him to call?" I couldn't answer. "Hey," she said, with suspicion in her voice, "who is this, anyway?"

"Just—a friend," I managed to say. My voice sounded thin, and I struggled to sound casual. "How long have you and Dave . . ."

"Been together?" She laughed softly. "A whole, scrumptious month!" She drew in her breath ecstatically. "Whoo-ee! Well, listen, I gotta run. I'm working the evening shift at Aces Hi. Any message for Dave?"

"I—no—" My pulse was pounding in my temples. "Yes—wait. Tell him his friend Misty called—Misty O'Brien."

I didn't remember hanging up the phone as I faced the wall in the garage. I stood there for a long time fighting

9

tears. I didn't want the mechanic to see me cry. Sharon's words reverberated in my mind. Living together? A month? How could it have happened? I saw Dave almost every day. I managed to write a check for the service, accepted an illegible carbon copy of work done, and walked to the car.

In the haven of my own little Camaro, I allowed the tears to ease the lump in my throat. I cried the three blocks to the apartment.

When I walked into the living room, despair pressed in on me like the atmosphere in a mortuary. Three days before I had been laid off from a job I loved as Administrative Assistant at the Sorensen Engineering Company. That job had required a B.A. degree and a hard year of on-the-job-training. I cried when my boss explained that with no new contracts, there wasn't enough money to keep all the employees. I wasn't the only one laid off, but that didn't help too much. I still had my share of apartment expenses to pay. And then, without warning, my roommate decided to get married, and took off. There wasn't a picture or a poster of hers left on the walls.

While losing my job and my roommate at the same time was financially devastating, they were blows I could handle. I had already landed a temporary job, and a friend was going to let me move in with her. But losing Dave—I couldn't cope with that. Could it have been a joke? Of course not. He couldn't have known I would call. Besides, he would never be that cruel.

Mechanically I began to pack my clothes. I worked steadily, trying to keep my mind blank. It took over an hour to get everything out of the closet and chest of drawers and into boxes and suitcases. I was trying to close the last suitcase when the phone rang. I let it ring. I didn't want to talk to anyone. On the sixth, shrill tone I finally picked up the receiver.

"Misty?"

My heart leaped at the sound of his voice. "Yes, Dave?" I forced myself to sound casual.

"Man! I've been waiting for you at the Sierra! Did you forget our date?"

"I didn't forget. I tried to call you."

I could almost hear his brain whirring as he realized what I'd said. After a long silence, he asked, "Do you still want me to come help you pack?"

"No, thanks," I said politely, and then I fell apart. "Who is she, Dave?" I screamed. "Your live-in maid?"

"I should have told you, Misty. I just couldn't find the right time." He cleared his throat. "I didn't want to hurt you."

"Didn't want to hurt me! Oh, Dave! I thought you loved me!"

"I do! Honest, I do!"

"Then why? Why?"

"Misty—I tried to tell you." His voice dropped to the husky tone that always thrilled me. "I do love you, baby. But—I have to have more."

I hung up on him, then fell across the bed. He had to have more! For months he had begged me to move in with him, but I had held out for marriage. "And what for!" I screamed at the walls. "Now I've lost him!"

I don't know how long I lay there, crying, reliving the past year, regretting, wondering about my values, and finally deciding what I had to do. I wasn't going to take that temporary job. I would leave Reno and go home to Stockton, to parents who loved me.

It took an hour to load the car, but at last I pulled away from the apartment house. Just before I left Reno I stopped at a phone booth, called my girl friend, and vaguely explained that something had happened and I had to rush home. Would she please explain to the man who was going to give me the job?

Now here I was in California, on the shoulder of Highway 80, about thirty miles west of Reno. *Oh, God,* I prayed. *What am I going to do?* How long had it been since I'd really prayed? Not since I'd fallen in love with Dave. How could I expect God to answer my prayer now? *But God! I can't live without him!*

Nevertheless I was living. At least my heart was still beating. Oh, if I could just die! Maybe suicide was the answer. But there were my stupid values again. I'd been brought up to believe suicide was a sin. I would have to go on living.

The headlights of passing cars illuminated a sign in front of me. Gradually its message penetrated my dull brain: A ROYAL REST AT THE ROYCE INN—DONNERVILLE, 5 MILES.

Maybe I ought to stop at that inn. I felt miserable. My eyes burned, my nose was hot and swollen, my mouth was dry, and I felt nauseated. I hadn't eaten anything since breakfast, and I suddenly realized I was hungry and exhausted. I started the car and pulled back onto the pavement. Five miles wouldn't be far.

I opened the window a crack and caught the scent of pine trees. The sound of the engine let me know I was climbing. In the distance I saw a red glow, and in a moment or two, in flowing script, the neon sign proclaimed, "THE ROYCE INN."

I slowed almost to a stop to turn in the driveway, where another sign signaled parking. I drove carefully through a narrow driveway between buildings which led to a lot at the back of the inn. The lot wasn't full, but I chose a small space and eased into it. With my overnight case in one hand and my sweater and purse in the other, I walked around the front. Although it was dark, I could see the lodge was built of logs, a huge, two-story building. Some of the dormer windows had lights, but for the most part, the hotel guests seemed to be asleep.

My legs felt heavy as I climbed the wide stairway which led to a veranda, and then crossed a carpeted area to a well-lighted lobby. My first impression was of old, polished elegance.

I felt a trace of light-headedness as I walked to the desk. It would be wonderful to lie down. Maybe I could even sleep a little while, and forget Dave—and Sharon. No one was at the desk, so I gave the bell a timid "ding." That was the last thing I remembered.

CHAPTER 2

ONCE BEFORE IN MY life I had fainted. It was the summer I was seventeen when a dentist had given me the opportunity to learn how to be a dental assistant. I enjoyed the work and was even learning how to do gold inlays, until I fainted one day during surgery. When I came to, I was sitting in a chair in the dentist's lab, and he was angry. "You picked a great time to pass out," he grated. He closed the door and left me alone. I was bewildered. I had no recollection of getting from the operating room to the lab.

Now, as I opened my eyes, I had the same sensation. I was lying down on a cold, leather couch. High, and directly overhead, was a gigantic wooden beam. How had I gotten here? Then I remembered. Dave. Sharon. I closed my eyes and wished I could slip into unconsciousness again. I knew I should make some effort to sit up and apologize to someone, but I was too tired to try.

"We've been over that before, Irene," I heard a man say. His voice was deep and resonant. "Now, please get this young woman something to drink. She should be coming

14

around soon." His voice seemed to be coming from behind me. I raised up on one elbow, then tentatively put my feet down on thick, red carpeting. Carefully I sat up and looked around. I saw a shapely woman in a black skirt and blue blouse disappearing through a darkened archway.

"Hello, there," the nice voice said. I looked up at a tall, slender man. He must have been over six feet tall. The light was wrong for me to see his features clearly, or the color of his eyes. But I could see they were brilliant and intense under heavy, black brows. His hair also seemed to be jet black, cut just above the earlobes and brushed back. He was wearing a brown leather jacket, which he now unzipped. He must have come in right behind me. He sat down on the couch and took my hands in his, and rubbed them. He smiled compassionately. "You're cold as ice." He picked up my sweater and put it around my shoulders. "You should have had this on. It gets cold at night in Donnerville." He stared at me for a moment. "Now tell me, are you ill? If you need a doctor, I can get one."

I held up my hand quickly and shook my head. "No, no. Really, I don't know why I fainted." I tried to smile. "I'm really quite a strong person."

"When did you eat last? You kids today starve yourselves."

Kids? He couldn't be much older than I. "That may be the problem," I admitted. "I haven't had anything to eat since breakfast."

"You see?" He shook his head. "You women are always dieting."

With his looks, I thought, he probably had plenty of women friends. He stood up. "I'm going out to the kitchen and see if I can get you something to eat. How about a sandwich?"

I smiled up at him. "Sounds good." Suddenly the

15

thought of food made me ravenous. I watched him stride toward the archway and hoped he would hurry. He turned lights on in the dining room and then disappeared behind swinging doors.

There were probably twenty white-clothed tables in the dining room, and from where I sat it seemed to be eighteenth-century elegance. The tall windows had red velvet, tasseled drapes, drawn back over white lace curtains.

I leaned back on the soft couch and looked around the lobby. The couch was several feet from the desk, and, as in the dentist's office so long ago, I wondered how I had gotten from there to here! Did the man carry me? I felt myself wincing at the thought. I must look a mess.

I reached in my purse for my compact, and I did look ghastly. In spite of a tan, my face was paper-white. My lipstick was gone, and my hair, which I usually wore pulled back, had come loose, and there were blond strings hanging down around my face. Quickly I took out the pins which held it, dug for a comb, and was just running it through the tangles when both the man and woman came back.

The woman—had he called her Irene?—held a tray with a sandwich and a glass of water, and although the man was smiling cordially, *her* face was like a still-shot of an unsmiling model. She had large, hazel eyes, which bored into mine. She wore a great deal of skillfully applied make-up and her eyebrows were tweezed and marked to perfection. Her auburn hair was in an upsweep, with shining curls on top. Full lips curved down petulantly. She wore several gold chains around her neck, perfectly graduated to match the deep cut of her blue satin blouse. I couldn't guess her age. She could be about my age— twenty-two—or she could be thirty. Regardless, she was a beautiful, stylish woman. In contrast, I felt embarrassed and ugly.

16

"Would you look at that," the man said. "She's got Alice-in-Wonderland hair!"

Irene placed the tray in front of me on a massive coffee table, and our eyes met for a dreadful moment. I eyed the sandwich hungrily. "Rubber chicken," she said, turned and walked through the door near the dining room.

I looked at the man inquiringly as he sat down beside me.

"Don't pay any attention to Irene," he whispered, grinning. "Eat."

"But what did she mean—rubber chicken?"

He laughed. "Hard egg sandwich!" He chuckled again as I doubtfully reached for half of the sandwich. "Irene used to be a waitress in Reno. She uses all that lingo."

"A waitress? She looks like a model."

"Yep. She's beautiful—and she can cook too!" A tiny crease appeared between his brows for an instant, then vanished. "I think we should get acquainted," he said. "I'm Dennis Parker. And who are you?"

"Misty O'Brien," I answered, as soon as I could after taking a big bite. The sandwich was the best I'd ever eaten! Of course I was starved, but it was no ordinary fried egg sandwich either. Irene had used some kind of exotic seasoning, and there were tiny bits of mushrooms and peppers in it. Besides that, the bread was homemade.

"What brings Alice-in-Wonderland to this godforsaken tourist trap?" Dennis asked, smiling. I looked down self-consciously, and he said, "Forgive me. I didn't mean to pry."

"That's all right," I said. I straightened slightly and lifted my chin. "Actually, I'm on my way to Stockton, and I became too tired to drive, so when I saw your sign—" I bit my lip. I could feel tears stinging my eyes. "I'm terribly sorry—and ashamed—that I fainted."

"Don't apologize." He leaned forward as though he

might touch me. "As manager of this . . ." he cleared his throat dramatically, "establishment—I've seen just about everything." He leaned back and smiled winningly. "But not many as lovely as you."

I gave him a scornful look. Who did he think he was kidding? I knew what I looked like. There was a twinkle in his eyes, which I could now see were royal blue. He was teasing me, probably trying to cheer me up. I realized he didn't mean I was all that beautiful, but it still made me feel better. He was charming. I liked him.

After I finished the sandwich and drank the water, I realized I was completely exhausted. "I would really like to get a room," I said. "Do I pay you now? And the sandwich . . ."

"Forget the sandwich," he said, as he stood up and walked toward the desk, "but you *will* have to register. You're in luck—I still have about twenty vacancies."

I reached down in my bag to get my billfold. Where was that wallet? I dumped everything out of my purse onto the couch. I pawed through brush, compact, keys, tissues—it was simply not there.

"Something wrong?" Dennis asked.

I fought down panic. "Oh—I guess my wallet is in the car." I scooped all the contents back in my purse and looked up at him. "Although I don't know how it could have fallen out—this flap is always over the top." I stood up. "I'll go look in my car."

"I'll go with you," he said, and together we went out into the cold mountain air, walked around the building and back to the Camaro. We both searched every inch of the car's interior, but it wasn't there. I had lost my wallet.

"It could only be in one of two places," I said. "I either left it at the garage when I paid my bill, or I left it in the apartment."

18

"Don't worry about it," Dennis said. "You can call in the morning, and pay us by check."

"No, I can't The checkbook is in the billfold. I've lost everything—I.D., credit cards—"

His eyes bored into mine, and there was no laughter there. He probably thought I was working some con game. We started back toward the entrance and I stopped just before we went inside. I drew myself up proudly. "I can't pay for the sandwich, and I won't be needing the room because I'm going back to Reno, but believe me, as soon as I can, I'll pay what I owe."

"Oh, come on, Alice-in-Wonderland—you're in no condition to drive." He took my arm firmly and guided me up the steps. "You're going to get a good night's sleep, and in the morning we'll tackle the case of the missing billfold."

A warning bell sounded in my mind, but I was so tired and disheartened I allowed him to propel me toward the lobby.

Irene stepped out of the dining room, and her beautiful face looked colder than ever. The look in her eyes was hostile. What was the matter? Why was she angry with me? Or was I imagining it?

"Sign the register, Misty," Dennis said as he turned the book toward me. "Irene, get the key for Seven." He smiled apologetically. "It's a small room, but away from the highway, so it'll be quieter." I signed my name and looked at him. He glanced at Irene, then down at me. "So. That takes care of that. Hope you sleep well." He turned abruptly and disappeared behind the wide, red-carpeted stairway. For the first time I noticed a discreet sign which read, "Cocktails." I saw a dimly lit opening, and the edge of what seemed to be a leather booth. If anyone else was in the bar besides Dennis, they weren't making any noise. I glanced at my watch. Midnight!

"I'll show you your room," Irene said. "Maybe we can all get some sleep tonight." I felt like an unwanted relative as I followed her up the stairs.

Number Seven was beside the stairwell, so I didn't have opportunity to look around before Irene opened the door and flipped on the light switch. She handed me the key, and without even a goodnight, she went down the hall toward the back of the building. In a moment I heard a door close.

I locked my door and looked around. The room was tiny, yet tastefully decorated in pale yellows and browns. There was a tiny closet and a tiny bathroom, and a not-so-tiny bed. It looked good to me. In a few minutes I was in my pajamas and in bed, staring wide-eyed at the ceiling.

CHAPTER 3

WHEN I AWOKE THE next morning my first thought was of Dave. Had it all been a nightmare? I raised to one elbow and looked around. No. The strange surroundings were evidence that Dave and I were through. I fell back against the pillow and closed my eyes. There was no reason to get up. No reason to live. I stayed in bed, absolutely still, trying to blot out all thoughts, perhaps even willing myself to die. But it was impossible to quit thinking. After a while I heard a man coughing in the next room. He sounded as though he might cough himself to death. The sound was disgusting! Irritably I threw back the covers and sat up. How could I keep my mind on this terrible crisis in my life with all that racket?

I went to the window and opened the drapes. Brilliant sunshine filled the room, warming everything it could reach. I couldn't see the highway, but I could hear constant traffic. A gardener under the window was doing something to the rosebushes. I could hear children playing. A dog barked. A motorcycle cracked and roared. How strange.

Life for other people was going on as usual, but my life was over.

I crossed over to the dresser and looked at my watch. Nine o'clock! I had to dress and get out of here. I dreaded the drive back to Reno. How could I have been so stupid as to leave my billfold? I could almost see it on the glass counter at the service station. Or was it still on that little chest of drawers at home? Did I have it when I used the telephone in that little market? I couldn't remember.

As I went into the bathroom to take a shower, I saw the telephone. For a moment I considered calling Dave. I could use the excuse that I needed him to call the service station for me. I lifted my chin and stepped into the tiny shower stall. Never! He didn't love me enough to wait until we were married. He was a cheater and a liar. If it killed me, I would never give him the opportunity to hurt me again. The stinging, hot shower made me think of the song, "I'm gonna wash that man right outa my hair." I tried to sing it, but the lump in my throat shut off the sound.

After I had dressed, combed my hair, and put on some make-up, I felt a little better. I wished I had brought in a change of clothes last night, but the stretch jeans still looked okay, and the lavender blouse was of a material that didn't wrinkle. I dug in my purse for a spray bottle of Cinnabar—Dave's favorite. I held it in my hand a moment, then tossed it into the wastebasket. I would never wear that scent again. I snapped shut the overnight case, picked up my sweater and purse, and glanced around. "Goodbye, little haven," I murmured. I picked up the key and walked downstairs.

Neither Dennis nor Irene was in sight as I came into the lobby. A man was standing at the switchboard—his back to me. My heart began to pound. Had Dennis told the morning clerk about me? If he hadn't, would he expect me to pay? I bit my lip. Could I sneak out? I glanced over toward the main door and the veranda beyond. Before I could move, the man turned around and saw me. He looked young, yet mature. There were a few lines around his eyes, which were light green and stared frankly into mine. He looked pleasant enough, and some of the tension eased out of my shoulders. His blond hair was parted on the side and came to his ears. It was full and clean-looking, with just the suggestion of a wave. He had on a blue-and-tan plaid shirt, open at the collar, and a tuft of blond hair stuck out impudently.

"Good morning." His voice matched his looks. I was tongue-tied as I placed the key on the counter. "Oh. You're number Seven," he said and smiled cordially. "Dennis told me about you. Why don't you come back here and sit down to do your telephoning." It was more of a command than a suggestion. I had already decided to drive back to Reno, but, like an obedient child, I walked around the end of the desk and stood beside him. Though he hadn't seemed tall on first impression, I felt shorter than my five-three standing next to him. He was at least six feet—maybe taller—and his chest and shoulders were broad. "Here, sit down right here, and use this phone," he ordered.

"I've decided to drive back to Reno—"

"No, no! Don't do that. Find out where you left the thing first. Then you can have them send it by United Parcel."

"Well—okay. But I'll pay for the calls." I took the service station bill from my purse and dialed their number.

"I'm in luck!" I told him a few minutes later. "I did leave my wallet on the counter when I paid for the car, and nobody noticed it until this morning! Can you believe it?" The desk clerk smiled and shook his head. "And fortunately for me, one of their customers is broken down about five miles from here, and, when the wrecker comes to get him, they'll bring me my billfold!"

23

"Sounds like you're in luck," he said. There was a teasing look in his eyes. "That is, if you believe in luck."

I shrugged. "He said it would probably be two hours before their mechanic gets here." I stood up and passed behind him. "Is it okay if I sit in the lobby to wait?"

"Why don't you go to the dining room and order some breakfast?" When he came out from behind the desk and stood beside me, I could smell his shaving lotion.

"But I don't—"

"—have any money," he finished, and took my arm. "I'll handle it. By the way, let me introduce myself. I'm Glenn Royce."

"Royce!" I echoed stupidly. "Then you must be the owner."

"Sad, but true."

"But I thought the man I met last night—"

"Dennis? He's the manager, and also my cousin." We walked into the dining room and he pulled out a chair for me. There was a red rose in a vase on every table. He sat opposite me, and turned slightly so he could keep an eye on the desk.

A tall, black girl who had been lounging against the cash register, strolled over to our table. She was dressed in a pink ruffled uniform which showed off lovely legs. Incongruously, she wore cowboy boots. Her dark face glowed like polished bronze, accentuating high cheekbones. Her eyes were large and soft under arched brows. There was a trace of good-natured arrogance in her manner as she dropped the menus in front of us.

"Hiya, Mr. Royce," she said. "You want breakfast or lunch?" She glanced at me and then back at Glenn.

"Coffee for me, Candy, and breakfast for the lady."

She looked at me with order pad and pencil ready. "You need more time?"

"No—just bring me an order of whole-wheat toast and a small glass of orange juice, please."

"Is that enough?" Glenn asked, and I nodded emphatically.

Candy wrote down the order, then turned, and with her head high and shoulders back, she walked proudly to the kitchen.

"This is only Candy's second day with us," Glenn volunteered. We watched her disappear behind the swinging doors. "She goes to U.C.L.A., but she and her boyfriend came through Donnerville at Eastertime. When they stopped here for lunch, Candy asked me if I ever needed help. So I hired her for the summer." He smiled widely, and I noticed his white, even teeth. He was really very nice-looking, but I had never been attracted to blond men. Dave was the epitome of everything I had ever looked for in a man. Tall, athletic, dark hair that turned to ringlets in the rain, blue eyes that became black and smoldering when aroused by my kisses . . .

"Dennis said she'd never come all this way from Los Angeles when school was out, but she did."

I had to struggle to pick up on the conversation. "She's pretty," I said.

"And intelligent," Glenn added. "She wants to get her B.A. degree in Personnel Management. That's probably why she was willing to work for the summer as a waitress. Undoubtedly her thesis will be something on the order of *Skills Needed for Unskilled Labor!*"

I laughed out loud. The sound startled me. How could I laugh at anything when my heart was broken? I sobered immediately. If Glenn wondered why, he was kind enough not to ask. It was a relief to see Candy return, and I smiled automatically.

With a flourish, she placed a silver-covered dish before

25

me, along with a frosted glass of orange juice. As I lifted the glass to my lips, Glenn stood up. He stretched slowly and thoroughly, and I couldn't help but notice his almost perfect build. He smiled down at me. "Listen, Seven, if you're still hungry after that enormous meal, just tell Candy, okay?"

"Aren't you going to drink your coffee?" Candy asked.

"I'll take it with me. I've got to get to work. Old Dennis has big plans to catch the tourist trade this summer, and I'm supposed to be checking out advertising." He picked up the coffee cup, left the saucer on the table, and took a few steps toward the lobby. He turned around and winked at me. "Enjoy your breakfast."

When he was out of sight, Candy remarked, "A really nice dude."

I smiled at her again. "He certainly seems nice." I lifted the silver cover and picked up a piece of warm toast. I bit into it, and the taste of melted butter and good bread was cheering. I looked around the dining room with a little more interest. "There doesn't seem to be much business," I observed.

Candy looked at her watch, then pulled out a chair to an adjacent table and sat down. "Most tourists get going before now." She brushed dust off her boots with a napkin. "But you're right. There's not much business. We only served about ten breakfasts this morning."

"I wonder why? It's a beautiful lodge."

"Too close to Reno," Candy said and pursed her lips wisely. "People are shooting for the big city and don't want to stop here. Or, if they're going the other way," she grinned, "they're broke!"

Suddenly Irene swept into the room on her way to the kitchen.

When she saw us, she called out, "Candy get your bod' in here. We're going to have one rotten day!"

Candy looked at me and shrugged. She uncrossed her legs, sighed, then stood up.

"What's wrong?" she shouted at the swinging doors.

Irene put her perfectly coiffed head around the door and glared at us. "That stupid hostess Mr. Royce hired is in the hospital with pneumonia, is what's wrong! I don't know how you and I can manage the lunch hour, much less dinner!"

She disappeared, and I looked up at Candy. "I thought there wasn't too much business?"

"I've only been here two days—but the waitress before me said lunch and dinner were heavy because this is the only nice place to eat in town." She tossed her head like an impatient race horse, and her golden, leaf-shaped earrings sparkled. "I'd better get back there and see what Her Highness wants me to do." She grinned wickedly, and I shook my head and smiled sympathetically.

I was just finishing my toast when Glenn came to the table and sat down. "How would you like to have a job?" he asked. Before I could answer, he said, "I know you're headed for home, but would a day or two make any difference?" I drew in my breath to answer, but he went on. "Our hostess has pneumonia, and although she's pretty sick, I'm sure she'll be okay in a few days. The problem is—Irene needs somebody right now." He looked at his watch. "In less than an hour the lunch trade begins, and we need someone to seat people, and to help Candy if she needs it. Think you could do that?" His green eyes looked pleading, and there was a pitiful frown between his brows.

"I suppose I *could*—but the only jobs I've ever had were office . . ."

"Will you do it?" he cut in urgently.

I frowned and bit my lip. I wanted to get as far from Reno as I could. But what difference did it make where I was? "Well—I'll try. But only for a day or two."

27

"Terrific!" Glenn said, rising. He called out, "Irene!" She came out of the kitchen with an impatient look on her face. Her hands were covered with flour. The effect was startling. It seemed to me she was the most unlikely person I'd ever seen to be the chef in a hotel. She walked toward him. "What is it?"

"Irene," Glenn said, smiling, "Miss O'Brien is going to be your hostess."

Her eyes widened, then narrowed. One eyebrow inched up, and her lips compressed into a straight line. This time I wasn't imagining. For some reason this woman hated me.

CHAPTER 4

THE INJUSTICE OF IRENE'S hateful attitude made me angry. What had I done to make her so hostile? I turned to tell Glenn I had changed my mind about accepting the job, but before I could speak, Irene sprayed me with questions. "Have you had any restaurant experience? Have you ever worked as a waitress? Why do you think you can be a hostess?"

For the first time since I found out about Dave and Sharon, I felt like fighting back. Who did this crab apple think she was anyway? I'm sure my gray eyes looked like cold steel when I said, "I, at least, have the ability to make people feel welcome!"

"Bravo!" Glenn whispered under his breath.

Irene rolled her eyes in exasperation. "It'll take more than that to be a hostess," she snapped, "but maybe you can learn." She gave Glenn a caustic look which he didn't see because he was beaming at me. He squeezed my arm. "Thanks, Misty. You'll do fine." I shrugged. I didn't care if I did or not. He went back to the lobby and Irene went to the kitchen. "Come on," she called over her shoulder.

In the kitchen Candy was cutting Irene's homemade pies into wedges. I had never been in a commercial kitchen before, and the size of the range and grill, as well as the sinks and dishwasher, amazed me. Above the stainless steel counters were shelves filled with huge cans of peaches, pears, corn, peas, and mixed vegetables. Although the floor was dark and old, it looked clean. Everything was neat and orderly. I didn't like Irene one bit, but I had to give her credit. She knew how to cook, and she knew how to manage a hotel kitchen. She was rolling out dough on a huge bread-board. I didn't know too much about cooking, so I assumed she was making more pie crust until she barked, "That stupid little skirt! If she hadn't gotten sick, I'd have these noodles done!" She rolled up the dough into a long cylinder, then with a sharp knife she began to slice it with vicious cuts. She glanced at me. "Okay—what was your name?"

"Misty O'Brien."

"Have you ever worked a cash register?"

"At Penney's, a couple of summers ago."

"At least thanks for that." She sighed impatiently. "Candy can show you how this one works. Now your job is to seat people. If it gets crowded, you have to put down their names in the order of arrival. Find out if they want smoking or non-smoking, give them menus, bring them water—and see that the glasses are dry on the outside so they won't make circles on the cloths—find out if they want coffee, and if they want it with or without, and serve it. Whenever you have any free time, don't stand around—help Candy."

"That's right!" Candy said, grinning at me. "I don't know where all the people come from, but from twelve o'clock to one around here it's a madhouse."

"Because the business people come in then." Irene retorted. By this time she had spread all the noodles out in neat rows. She glanced up at a wall clock and swore. "I don't know if there's time for these to get done for the special!" She carefully placed them in a huge pot, which was simmering with a good-smelling chicken broth. "Candy, take her out front and show her where everything is. Show her how to make a set-up, and tell her about the salad. Get the lead out, will you?"

In the dining room I remembered I was wearing jeans. "I've got to change clothes," I said.

"You ain't got da time," Candy said, sounding like the Tar Baby in the "Uncle Remus" stories my mother used to read to me. She had an amusing, yet disconcerting way of switching from King's English to the dialect of a southern slave.

"But jeans?"

"Sure. Anything's okay here in the mountains."

I don't know if any of the men who crowded in for lunch noticed my clothes, but there was one table of six women who stared at me with disapproval. We were so busy, though, I didn't have time to feel self-conscious. About two o'clock it was all over, and Candy and I both flopped in chairs, legs stretched out, and arms hanging down at our sides. We grinned at each other. "You did good!" she exclaimed, and I felt pleased.

The happy feeling didn't last long though, because Irene began to tell me all the things I did wrong—I talked too much to the patrons—I didn't notice when people needed more water or coffee—I kept an important man waiting. If it hadn't been for the fact that both the owner and the manager of this inn had been so kind to me I would have walked out. But I took her criticism.

By four-thirty, after I had showered and changed into a dress, I was over my resentment and was looking forward to the evening trade. Who would come to dinner? Would we have many tourists? Most importantly, could I handle it?

I had a mild case of stage fright when I came down the stairs wearing a pale blue silky dress, with soft ruffles over the arms, and another ruffle down the side of the skirt. I had loved the dress when I first saw it, and had bought it because blue was Dave's favorite color. My hair was coiled high on my head and held in place with a sparkling comb. I had put on more eye make-up than usual, probably to bolster my courage. It made me look older and more sophisticated, and I hoped Irene would realize that I was not to be disciplined as a child.

Dennis was at the desk and when he turned and saw me, his look of genuine admiration gave a much-needed boost to my ego.

"Alice!" he whispered. He came around the desk and took my hands. "You're lovely!"

I smiled up at him. "Is this dress all right for host-essing?"

"The only problem with that dress is that it might make all the male diners forget their hunger, thereby causing Royce Inn to lose money on the dinner trade." He gave me a long, appreciative look that made me blush with pleasure. I couldn't remember Dave ever saying complimentary things, or looking at me like that. Surely he had, but he was not one to praise people as a general rule.

"By the way," Dennis said, dropping my hands, and turning back to the desk. "A fellow from that service station in Reno brought your wallet." He reached under the counter and handed it to me.

"Oh!" I opened it quickly to see if everything was in it. "Now I can pay you!" I began to write a check. Dennis put his hand over mine. "Let's wait until we figure out what we owe *you*. When you leave, we can get it all straightened out." He didn't move his hand, and it felt large and warm over mine. At that moment Irene stepped out of the dining room. Her unblinking eyes reminded me of a vampire I had seen in a horror movie. My heart began to pound and I withdrew my hand quickly.

"Hi, Irene," Dennis said without smiling. "Can I do something for you?"

"Yes. You can tell the new employee it's time to go to work." She looked past me as though I wasn't there, whirled around, and stalked back to the kitchen.

CHAPTER 5

I STARED AT IRENE'S back until she was out of sight, then looked at Dennis. "Why does she dislike me so much?"

For a second or two his eyes smoldered with anger, then he laughed. "Don't pay any attention to Irene! She doesn't dislike you. She just thinks every new woman on the scene is a threat."

"Threat? To what?"

"Her importance—" he pursed his lips as though he had said too much, but he finished the sentence, "to Glenn and me."

"Well, she certainly needn't worry about me! Tomorrow I'll be on my way to Stockton." I was angry and regretted ever taking the job. I took a deep breath, squared my shoulders, and started toward the dining room.

In a flash Dennis was around the desk and put his warm hand on my arm.

"You can't leave tomorrow!" His eyes were serious and his expression urgent. "I visited Jean—the hostess—in the hospital this afternoon. There's no way she can come back to work for at least a week—probably longer."

"I'm sorry, Dennis." I had to look away from his eyes to concentrate on what I was saying. "Glenn said the job would only be for a day or two. Anyway I'm sure there's someone here in Donnerville who would be more to Irene's liking." I walked away quickly and almost ran into Candy as I entered the dining room.

"Hi, babe. What's up? You look like you had a run-in with your worst enemy."

I wanted to confide in Candy and was reasonably sure she felt as I did about Irene. But in my freshman year at college, I had learned the hard way not to talk about people. Every time I said something bad about someone, it always boomeranged. I tried to smile. "Nerves, I guess. Hope I do better tonight than I did today."

"You did great! I already told you that." Candy's big eyes were soft and friendly.

"Not according to Irene," I said, hoping Candy would say something ugly about her, yet ashamed of myself for such a thought.

"Listen, one thing you got to learn—don't let her get to you. She doesn't have the authority. As long as you please the bossmen, you gonna be okay!" She glanced at the kitchen doors, then smiled slyly. "And it seems to me, you're pretty pleasing to Mr. Parker!"

"Mister who?" I asked brainlessly. I could feel color rising in my face.

"Dennis Parker, dopey. The good-looking one."

Before I had to make a comment, there was a commotion behind us, and we turned to watch a large group of men and women as they crossed the red-carpeted lobby toward the dining room. "Oh, oh!" Candy whispered. "Looks like it's time to go to work."

For a moment I felt like running away, but I smiled and stepped forward to greet them. "How many?" I asked. My voice sounded so calm it amazed me.

"Twelve, baby," the spokesman said. "Hey, where did Glenn ever find you?" His lecherous inspection practically undressed me. He leaned over and whispered, "When do you get off work, baby?" The sickening smell of alcohol billowed out with each word and I stepped back involuntarily.

"I'm working the twenty-four-hour shift," I replied, in a bantering tone. I turned and led them to the biggest table, back by the windows. Before I could bring menus, several more people came in.

"Must be some kind of shindig going on tonight," Candy murmured under her breath as she pranced by me with a tray of tinkling water glasses held high on one hand. In a short time every table was filled, and several more people were waiting, either in the lobby or at the bar.

For the next three hours I raced from the cash register to the kitchen, from the kitchen to the tables, and back to the cash register, trying to do everything Candy and Irene told me to do. Finally, when everyone was gone except for a few stragglers who were lingering over after-dinner coffee, I went to the kitchen.

"When those customers out there leave, is it okay if I get something to eat?" I asked Irene. Her back was turned as she scolded the busboys about something, and she didn't answer right away. I was just turning to go back into the dining room when she called over her shoulder. "Sure. You're entitled to eat anything and as much as you want."

"Were there any of those noodles left from lunch?" I asked. For the first time she looked at me with a semi-pleasant expression on her face. "You like homemade noodles?"

36

"Yes, I do," I said. "My mother makes them, but it's been a long time since I've eaten any."

Irene clicked on high heels over to the enormous refrigerator and took out a small plastic container. "There's just about enough here for a good helping. I'll put it in the micro."

"Not yet," I said. "There are still some people out there who haven't paid their checks."

She waved me to a chair by a big wooden table. "I'll take care of them. Eat whatever you want." Without looking back, she went out to the dining room, as cool and lovely as a spring bouquet.

I walked over to the steam stable and looked at what was left of the entrées. I could have Swiss steak, or turkey or veal scallopini. I had heard Irene tell some patron, "Of course I use veal in the veal scallopini. Nothing but the best is served at Royce Inn." It did look good, and would go well with the noodles. I was hungry! I walked over to where the busboys were sullenly loading the dishwasher. "Excuse me, but would you hand me a plate, please?"

The tallest one reached over to a rack of clean dishes, then gave me a heavy plate.

"What's your name?" I asked.

"Bret," he said and smiled. "And that's Rick." Rick looked up and nodded.

"You fellows worked here long?"

"Nope," Bret answered. "Nobody has." He suddenly seemed friendly and talkative. "See, when the old Mr. Royce was alive, he never had the dining room open—at least not as long as I can remember. But Mr. Parker—he's the one who got it going."

"The whole town's jazzed over it," Rick added.

"Yeah, cause the only other place around here to eat is McDonald's or the Open Kitchen."

37

"And a person would have to be sick to eat there."

"You mean he'd be sick *after* he ate there," Bret said, making a horrible gagging noise which almost made me lose my appetite.

I walked over to the steam table and put a small piece of veal on my plate, then opened the microwave oven and took out the noodles. "You fellows like your jobs?"

They looked at each other, then smiled sarcastically. "It's a job," Bret said.

"It would be okay if it weren't for Frankenstein's bride," Rick added. Both boys laughed.

I started to give my opinion about Irene, then stifled my words. After all, I didn't need to discuss her with a couple of teen-age boys. What did she matter to me? By this time tomorrow night I'd be in Stockton. I suddenly felt weary and sad. Even the thought of seeing my parents didn't matter. The only thing that really mattered to me was Dave. Where was he tonight? What was he doing? Did he miss me?

I got some salad and a piece of garlic bread and sat down at the table, which was several feet away from the boys. I don't know if Bret didn't think I could hear, or if he had forgotten me, but he said, "Rick, you'd better watch your mouth about her. She could get you fired."

"She's not my boss," Rick retorted. "Mr. Parker hired us."

"Yeah—but guess who I saw last night when I dumped the garbage?"

"Who?"

"Mr. Parker and her."

"Oh, yeah? So?"

"So they were sittin' in his car—and, brother, they weren't discussin' menus."

38

CHAPTER 6

UNEXPECTEDLY THE MENTAL PICTURE of Dennis and Irene locked in an embrace in the front seat of his car, hurt me. It was a "last-straw" feeling and I wanted to cry, but I continued to chew and swallow, even though the food had lost its flavor. No wonder Irene was hateful toward me. Dennis had been attentive and complimentary, and she was jealous. Now *I* was feeling something akin to jealousy! But what had I expected? The first time I saw him I figured he would have lots of women friends.

I stood up and dumped what was left on my plate into a huge galvanized trash can. I handed my plate to Bret. "Sorry!" I said lightly. "Man's work is never done!" Then I walked quickly across the kitchen, through the swinging doors, and into the dining room. I hadn't seen Glenn since morning, but Dennis had done a little table-hopping during the dinner hour, and I knew he was on duty at the desk. With a little speed, maybe I could dash up the stairs without his seeing me. I'd pack, take a shower, get a good night's rest, and be on my way home early in the morning.

"Hey!" Candy's voice stopped me and I turned to look at her. She was sprawled out at one of the tables drinking something from a tall glass. "Come here." Sometimes I resented her authoritative tone of voice and this was one of those times. "I'm tired," I said. "I'm going to bed."

"To bed!" She leaned back and studied one of the beams in the ceiling. "I thought maybe you and I could go out on the town."

"This town?" I smirked. "Like what?"

"We could go bowling." She looked at me for encouragement. "Or roller skating." I shrugged. She swirled her drink, then took a swallow. "How about hitting a few bars?"

"Sorry, Candy. In the first place, I'm exhausted; and in the second place, I don't drink." I started toward the lobby. "But if I wasn't going home tomorrow, I'd take you up on the roller-skating."

"You is boun' and determined to leave po' li'l me a slave in de hands of dese cruel white folks!"

"Oh, Candy!" I walked back and hugged her. The smell of alcohol surprised me—although it shouldn't have. Almost everyone I had known at Sorensen drank. "You'll never be anyone's slave!" I said. "Give me your pen and ticket book. I want to give you my home telephone number so, when you come through Stockton, you can call. We'll get together sometime."

She took the tablet and pen out of her uniform pocket. "First," she said, "let me give you my extension here." She scribbled a few numbers. "You may change your mind and call me before the night's over."

"Don't count on it." I took the little piece of paper, then wrote my name and parents' address and telephone number on the back of another ticket and handed it to her. "If I don't see you in the morning, thanks for trying to teach me how to be a hostess."

40

"I sure wish you were staying," she said. Her luminous eyes looked suspiciously moist, and her lower lip trembled. I whirled around and left the dining room before either of us could get too sentimental.

Irene was behind the desk, seated next to Dennis. Her face, in profile, was lovely. She looked like a woman in love. Neither of them noticed me as I scooted quietly up the stairs.

In number Seven I sat down on the bed. I still couldn't fathom my feelings about Dennis and Irene. I loved Dave! Didn't I? What did it matter what Dennis, or any other man, did? And yet, he had been so nice to me! He had made me feel desirable.

I unzipped my dress, took it off, and folded it carefully. Fortunately I hadn't brought in all my luggage, so there wasn't a lot to pack. In a few moments I had everything back in the suitcases, except for a clean pair of faded jeans, a comfortable western shirt, lingerie, and pajamas. As I worked I kept going over the conversation I'd overheard between Rick and Bret, and some things Dennis had said to me. I sucked in my breath and let it out. I was sick and tired of thinking about life—and love. I honestly, sincerely, wished I could die and be done with it!

The tiny shower stall was cold, and goosebumps popped out all over me as I stood on the icy tile waiting for the hot water to come. I took a long shower and some of the tension left my shoulders under the needles of hot water. By the time I had dried my hair, I was sleepy. In fact, I couldn't wait to get in bed, because I didn't feel very good. I remembered how I had felt just the night before, and wondered if perhaps I had picked up some kind of bug. My back ached as I snuggled under the covers and my throat felt just a little scratchy, but I was in a deep sleep before I had time to think any more about it.

41

When I awoke the next morning, my throat was more than a little scratchy. It hurt to swallow and I felt hot. "Too bad, Misty," I croaked, trying out my voice. "No matter how you feel, you can't stay here. So get dressed."

When I stood up everything whirled, and I had to sit back down on the bed. I felt horrible! I hadn't felt so wretched since I had German measles in my senior year in high school. There was no doubt about it—I had something and it was serious enough to keep me from driving. What rotten luck! I fell back on the pillow and groaned. What could I do? I could call my mother. Maybe she and Dad would come get me. I looked at my watch. Seven o-clock. Good. Daddy didn't leave for work until seven-thirty. I sat up and with my head spinning, I got an outside line and dialed home. As I waited for the phone to ring, I wondered if Glenn was on the switchboard. Apparently he took the morning shift at the desk, and Dennis, the evening. After about fifteen rings I hung up. Where could they be? I dialed again, but still no answer. Alarmed, I dug in my overnight bag for my address book. I would call the Browns, our next-door neighbors.

"Misty!" Mrs. Brown's warm voice told me she was pleased to hear from me. "Are you in Reno?"

"No—I'm on my way home. Do you know why my parents don't answer the phone?"

"I sure do! Your mom had a chance to go with your dad on a business trip to Dallas. She tried all yesterday afternoon to call you!"

"Really?" My shoulders sagged with disappointment. I sighed. "When will they be home?"

"Two weeks from yesterday. Can I do anything for you, dear?"

I couldn't ask her to drive up and get me—anyway, even if she was willing, what could we do with my car? I decided

I wouldn't even tell her I was sick. Why worry her?

"No—not really. I just changed plans for the summer. Do you know where they'll be staying in Dallas?"

She gave me the number. I thanked her and hung up. So much for that idea. I lay down, then realized I was also getting sick at my stomach.

Afterward, shivering and miserable, I crept into bed and went to sleep for a while. When I awoke I was burning hot and knew I had to have some help. I thought of Candy and felt around in my bag until I found the ticket with her telephone number on it.

"Candice, here," she said in a phony British accent.

"Candy—it's Misty. I'm sick. Can you come to my room?"

"Be right there. Unlock your door."

When Candy knocked lightly on the door, then opened it, I was surprised and embarrassed to see Glenn with her. He was wearing a brown suit, white shirt, and a brown knit tie. Both of them looked worried and concerned. Glenn came directly to the bed and sat down beside me. He put his hand on my forehead. "I think you have a temperature," he said. Candy looked so anxious that, if my head hadn't been pounding, I would have laughed. "Think I'll call Doc Davis," Glenn said.

"Oh, please don't," I whispered. "I'm not that sick."

"You may not be. But on the other hand, I think you need medication. Doc Davis will know what to do." He turned around to look at Candy. "You'd better not stay. If she has something contagious—"

"I never get sick," she boasted.

"You go down to the switchboard and you'll find Doc's telephone number on that card of emergency numbers."

Candy motioned to the telephone. "Why don't you just call from here?"

43

"Because nobody's on the switchboard right now. Dennis doesn't come on duty until ten-thirty. If Doc's not home, try the Elks Club. He goes there on Sunday mornings."

Sunday morning! I had been so wrapped up in my own problems, I hadn't even remembered what day it was. Then I noticed that Glenn was wearing a suit. Was he planning to go to church?

When Candy left the room, Glenn got a glass of water from the bathroom. "Here, drink this." He put his hand under my shoulders and lifted me up, then held the glass to my lips. "It may not stay down," I said, taking only a sip at a time.

"Stomach upset too?" He shook his head in sympathy. I drank about half of the water, then he eased me back down on the pillow. When he leaned over me, I noticed the nice scent of his shaving lotion again. I looked up into his green eyes. "Did Candy tell you I was sick?"

"Nope." He smiled down at me, then pulled a chair over close to the bed and sat down. "When you picked up the phone this morning, I was on the switchboard. I thought your voice sounded peculiar, and since you had fainted the night before, I was worried about you. I don't make a practice of eavesdropping, but I listened to your conversation with Candy."

I felt I should make some reply, but I was too miserable. My eyes ached, so I had to close them, and I turned slightly in order to ease the pain in the small of my back.

"Poor girl," Glenn sympathized. "You do feel awful, don't you?"

When Candy came back, Glenn stood. "Did you get him?"

"Yes." Candy's voice sounded professional. "He'll be here as soon as he can."

"Do you mind waiting for him, then bringing him up here?"

"Of course not."

"Dennis will be at the switchboard in about five minutes. I'd wait for Doc myself, but I'm supposed to give the message this morning."

So he *was* dressed for church. And he was going to preach. Strange. He didn't look like a preacher.

I heard the door close and felt both relief and anxiety. It was a miserable feeling to be sick in front of strangers—to be in pajamas, with no make-up on, your hair a mess, and your teeth not brushed. But it was worse to be sick in strange surroundings—all alone.

CHAPTER 7

A LIGHT KNOCK ON the door startled me. It seemed as though I had been asleep for a long time, but it must have only been minutes. Candy was beside my bed, saying, "Here's the doctor, Misty."

Dr. Davis was stocky with unruly, almost orange hair. His eyes were merry, and pale blue under wiry eyebrows.

"You *must* be sick, young lady," he said with a chuckle, as he shook the thermometer, "to be willing to stay *here*. Right, Dennis?"

I turned my head quickly. Dennis stood by the door with a grave expression on his face. "Just make her well, Doc. We don't need your levity this morning."

Dr. Davis winked at me and put the thermometer in my mouth. Candy came to the bed and touched my arm.

"I have to go to work now, but I'll come see you as soon as the rush is over."

I wanted to tell her I was sorry to cause all the trouble, but I didn't think the doctor would appreciate my taking the thermometer out of my mouth. I nodded my head and tried to smile. She waved and slipped out the door. Dennis moved closer to the bed. "I'll bet you had this bug night before last," he said. I closed my eyes to shut out his penetrating gaze. I felt so ashamed to think I had probably infected a lot of people. After what seemed an unnecessary length of time, Dr. Davis took the thermometer.

"Hundred and one," he said. "Not too bad."

"What is it?" Dennis asked.

"Without running tests, I can't say—but I'll wager it's nothing to be alarmed about. I'll give her some antibiotics and she'll be okay in no time." He patted my arm. "Is there any kind of medication you're allergic to?"

"Not that I know of."

"Good." He reached into his bag and prepared an injection. I watched apprehensively as he squeezed a drop out of the needle. "Where do you want it?" I saw Dennis smile, and either my temperature began to rise, or I was blushing. "In my arm," I murmured.

Afterward, he scribbled a prescription and handed it to Dennis. Then he looked at me. "I want you to take every last one of those pills, you hear?" He snapped shut his case, then stood up. "Can't understand why people call me, then don't take the medicine I prescribe." He held out his hand to Dennis. "Take care of her—make her stay in bed." He glanced back at me as they shook hands. "She's a cute thing."

After Dennis closed the door, he came to the bed and sat down. I was painfully conscious of his nearness, and my unattractive condition. Why had he come anyway?

"Do you feel any better?" His voice was low and tender.

"I think I do. At least better than a couple of hours ago."

He held up the prescription.

"I'll run down to the drugstore and get this filled right away."

"Shouldn't you be at the desk?" I asked.

He smiled broadly. "Hey! I think Alice is feeling better!" He leaned toward me and put his hand on my cheek. "She's worrying about the store!" He moved his hand slightly until it rested on my throat. I was startled at his familiarity—and my response! In spite of my sickness, this man held some kind of fascination for me. I felt ashamed, and moved away slightly. He moved his hand then and became more business-like. "Yes, I've agreed to cover for Glenn on Sunday mornings so he can . . ." he assumed a saintly pose, and his voice took on a mournful tone, "worship the Lord." I had to smile. "But just about everyone has checked out, and there won't be any business now until church is over—except for a couple of barflies, and Irene can handle them."

"Who is going to hostess today?" I asked.

"Glenn called one of the gals here in town—Debbie Harlan. Her aunt owns the souvenir shop, and Deb usually works for her. But there's not that much going on in town right now, so she said she would help out for a day or two, until we either hire someone or until Jean comes back." I nodded, then turned to look at the window. "Why?" Dennis put a finger under my chin and turned my face back toward him. "Why?" he asked again. "Did you change your mind about working at Ye Olde Royce Inn?"

It was a mistake to look into his eyes. Those sapphire-blue pools hypnotized me, and I couldn't think. I don't know how long I stared at him, while a wonderful sensation, like the plunging of a swing, rippled inside me. I felt him take my hand, and I made no protest.

"I know now why you got sick, little Alice." His voice was deep and tender. "In your subconscious, you really wanted to stay."

I finally came out of the trance I was in. "No, I did *not*

want to stay!" I could feel my mouth getting prim. "I have no desire to work for Irene. However, I did learn just this morning that my parents are not home, and if it would help you and Glenn, I would be glad to work another ten days."

"Fantastic!" he chortled, getting to his feet. "I can't wait to tell Glenn—and Irene."

I smiled apologetically. "Irene won't be glad. I don't know why she dislikes me so—" I gave him a significant look. I thought about what Bret had said and wondered if I really wanted to stay here for another ten days. But I certainly didn't want to stay in Stockton alone, and I would not go back to Reno.

"Like I told you yesterday—don't pay any attention to her. She'd find something wrong with the maitre d' at the Hilton. The thing now is to get you well." He leaned over and kissed my forehead. "I believe you're cooler." He grinned boyishly and waved the prescription. "I'll get this filled and start pouring chicken soup down your throat!" In two easy strides, he was out the door. He blew me a kiss and was gone.

I didn't know what the doctor had given me, but I was already feeling better. I sat up and put both pillows to my back. I didn't feel dizzy and not the least bit nauseated. If only I had something to read. But I didn't. I had a lot of reading material in the Camaro, but the only thing in the room was a telephone book.

I got out of bed and turned on the television. I could only get three channels. Two of them had so much snow I couldn't enjoy watching; and the third, with good reception, showed the closing moments of a church service. I got back in bed and listened to the preacher. He was an earnest-appearing, balding man of forty or so. When the camera came in for a close-up, I could see tiny beads of sweat on his upper lip. His voice was almost a wail.

"No matter how far you've strayed, no matter what sins you've committed, Jesus is waiting for you to come back to Him. The choir is going to sing that old favorite, 'Softly and Tenderly—Jesus Is Calling.' If you've strayed away, come back. Come back to Jesus while there is still time."

I listened as the choir sang, and a strange longing crept over me. Maybe it was nostalgia, but I felt like crying. I got up and snapped off the set. When I got back in bed I thought of Glenn, and wondered what kind of a sermon he had preached this morning. I would like to hear him. Maybe next Sunday I could.

I sighed deeply and leaned back into the pillows. It was such a relief to feel better. I decided to brush my teeth and wash my face. "And do something with this hair," I mumbled, when I saw myself in the bathroom mirror. There were dark circles under my eyes, and for a moment I felt so dizzy I had to hang onto the wash basin. But I brushed my hair, then braided it, fastening the ends with rubber bands.

I opened the big suitcase and took out some mint green lounging pajamas that Mother had given me for Christmas. I had never had a reason to wear them, but this seemed the perfect time. I had to stay in bed and rest, yet I wanted to be presentable. I shook them out and spread them on the bed. Mother usually bought expensive things for her "baby," and these were no exception. The material felt like silk, yet didn't wrinkle. There were lace insets across the shoulders, and the short sleeves were trimmed in lace. I got out of my other p.j.'s and put on the green ones. They fit perfectly, and I was pleased that they were opaque enough to be modest, yet feminine and soft.

I straightened up the bed, then lay down on top of the bedspread. I dozed, and was awakened by a soft knock and the sound of Glenn's voice.

"May I come in, Misty?"

"Yes, just a minute." I crossed to the door and unlocked it. "Come in." I tottered slightly, and he grabbed my arm.

"Still not feeling too super, are you?" he said.

I sat on the bed. "I'm much, much better. Just a little dizzy, but I think I'm practically well—thanks to your Dr. Davis."

"He's a pretty good doctor," Glenn said, and sat down in a chair.

We smiled at each other. "How was church?" I asked.

"Fine—I guess."

"I was wondering if I might go with you next Sunday—oh, did Dennis tell you I was staying a few more days? That is, if you want me?"

Glenn nodded, smiling brightly. "Yes, he told me. We're both glad."

"So since I'll be here next Sunday, I'd like to hear you preach."

"Thanks, but I'm not scheduled for next Sunday. It's a small work, and there are three of us who alternate giving the message." His eyes were sparkling, and it was evident that the church was important to him. "I'd be glad to take you with me though. Jack Prather will be speaking. He's a good man."

"How did you get started preaching? Did you volunteer, or what?"

He laughed and shook his head. "I guess you could say I volunteered. I've been going to that church since I was in high school. In fact, it was at one of the young people's meetings that I felt the call to become a preacher."

I leaned back against the pillow. I must have sighed or looked pale, because Glenn jumped to his feet and hurried to the bed. "What's wrong?" His eyes were wide and his eyebrows furrowed.

"Nothing—why?"

"I thought you were going to faint again. Have you had anything to eat?"

I shook my head. "I'm not hungry. I don't think I could eat anything."

"Did the water stay down?" he asked.

"Yes, but—"

"I think you need something. I'm going to bring you some hot soup. Irene will have something delicious. She always does on Sundays." He touched my forehead. "I do believe your temperature is down. We can thank God for that!"

"I hate for you to have to bring soup up here. Maybe I can go downstairs."

"No you can't—at least, not now. Remember how dizzy you were a few moments ago?" He took my hand and patted it. "You just stay right here and Uncle Glenn will bring you some good soup, okay?" When he smiled his teeth glistened and sparkled. I'd never known anyone with such a brilliant smile.

"Tell you what," he said. "Dennis and I trade shifts on Sundays, so that I can go to church, and it gives him a night off. If you're feeling a lot better tonight, you can come down to the desk and sit with me for a while."

Last Sunday night Dave and I had gone to see "Fiddler on the Roof" in one of the dinner theaters. *Oh Dave, my darling. I miss you so.*

I tried to smile at Glenn. "If my temperature is normal, I'll be glad to."

CHAPTER 8

GLENN HAD BEEN GONE about half an hour when I heard someone knock. I walked carefully to the door, then called, "Who is it?"

"I have some soup for you." I didn't recognize the musical, feminine voice, but I opened the door a crack. An attractive girl about my age, with a mass of wild, red, curly hair smiled at me. I opened the door wider and stepped back.

"Hi!" she said, breezing into the room. "I'm Debbie Harlan. Glenn and Dennis are in some big confab with a guy from Reno, and they wanted me to bring you the soup and medicine." She put a tray on the dresser. A silver cover hid the bowl, but a large, plastic prescription container sat solidly on the tray in plain sight. I wondered how much all that medicine had cost.

"Thank you." I felt light-headed again, so I sat down on the bed. I smiled up at her. "Dennis told me you were hostessing today."

"Yeah—well—sort of!" She flipped her curly hair back

53

and grinned like a pixie. "I'll probably have the customers so confused they'll never come back."

I laughed, then motioned toward a chair. "Have a seat."

"No, I can't stay—there are still people coming in." She stepped through the door. "Take care—I'll see you later. You want the door locked?"

I shrugged. "I guess so. Thanks again for bringing my dinner."

"No problem!" She waved, and closed the door.

I took the cover off the soup. It smelled good—some kind of beef broth with vegetables in it. There were also some oyster crackers in a cellophane bag. I opened the package and put one of the round saltines in my mouth. It tasted delicious. I poured the rest of them in the soup, sat down in the chair, and ate every morsel. While I wiped my lips with the large linen napkin, I picked up the prescription bottle and began to read: "Misty O'Brien. One tablet daily at bedtime. No refills." I hoped I wouldn't need a refill! In fact, after I had eaten, I felt almost like my old, healthy self. Maybe I could dress and go downstairs. Yet, Dr. Davis had said to stay in bed. I went to the bathroom, brushed my teeth, and drank some water. Then I got back into bed and went to sleep.

When I awoke, the room was almost dark. I sat up and looked out the window. The sun was gone and the sky was a deep purple. I snapped on the lamp and looked at my watch. Almost seven o'clock! I don't know whether it was the purple sky or being in a strange room, but I felt lonely and neglected. Where was everybody? Didn't Candy say she would come see me this afternoon? Glenn had said he would bring the soup—and then he sent a stranger. And what had happened to Dennis? He was going to get the prescription himself and bring it to me. I walked to the window and closed the drapes. A person could die here and no one would care. Besides that, I was hungry! Well, I didn't need them. I felt just fine! I decided to dress, and if I could get past Glenn, I would get in the car and find that McDonald's Bret had mentioned. I certainly didn't want to risk Irene's wrath by asking for something from her kitchen.

I dressed in jeans and a sleeveless blouse. I had bought the blouse three years before, but I loved it and kept wearing it every summer. It was made of white eyelet, and had a ruffle around the scoop neck. I took my hair out of braids, and after a thorough brushing, it billowed out around my shoulders. I wasn't in the mood to put on a lot of make-up, and just touched my lips with gloss. I had my purse and key in my hand and was about to go out the door when I remembered Dennis saying that it gets cold at night in Donnerville. I got a white sweater out of the suitcase, then with a quick look-around, I left number Seven.

I was almost down the stairs when Glenn rushed up, taking two at a time. He tried to stop before running into me, but we both staggered, and I found myself pushed back on a step, looking up into his startled face.

"Misty! Man! I'm so sorry." He pulled me to my feet. "I was just coming up to see you. Are you all right?"

"I'm fine—I think!" I shook my head in wonder. "Do you always go up the stairs like that?"

He took my arm and we walked sedately down the remaining steps and into the lobby. "No, but I've been trying all afternoon to find a moment when I could check on you, and there's just been one thing after another."

His blond hair was slightly mussed, and his fresh white shirt of the morning was rumpled, and open at the collar. "Are you really as well as you look?"

"Yes! In fact, I'm hungry—"

"How could you recover so quickly?" He cocked his head and squinted at me.

"I'm sure the shot helped, but I've about decided I must have had some twenty-four hour thing."

"It's good to see you up—but I hope it's not too soon."

"I'm fine! Really! I'm on my way to McDonald's to get a hamburger and a malt." I expected him to protest, but instead his eyebrows shot up and he grinned. "Great idea!" He reached for his billfold. "I haven't had a hamburger for a month. Get me some French fries, too, will you? And a large Coke." He handed me a twenty-dollar bill. My mouth must have been hanging open because he added, "I'd go with you, but I can't leave the desk."

The food smelled so good on the way back I couldn't resist eating a couple of Glenn's fries. As soon as I walked in the lobby he was on his feet, grinning.

"I'm starved! Come on back here." He pulled out a steno chair for me to sit on, and he perched on a stool in front of the switchboard. I put the sack down, then counted out his change. He started to take it, then said, "Wait a minute." He opened the sack, took out the hamburgers, fries, and drinks. "This much food cost more than that! What did you do—pay for your own?" His voice was controlled but tense, and his eyes looked dark for a moment. "I intended to buy yours."

I shook my head firmly. "No, no. I already owe you too much. The room, my meals, and the medicine—the doctor!" I raised my hands and let them fall. "In fact, I want you to figure out everything and let's get it straight tonight. Please. I'd feel a lot better about it."

He shrugged, then smiled brightly. I don't know if it was his white teeth, or his eyes, or his tan, but when he smiled his whole face seemed to light up. "Okay, whatever," he agreed. "Let's eat!" He took my hand and closed his eyes. "Heavenly Father, thank you for this food, and, Lord, thanks that Misty is feeling so much better. Amen." He took a bite and said, "Mmm! Good! Did you bring any catsup for the fries?"

I nodded, and handed him the little packages. For some reason it made me happy that I remembered to get extra catsup.

We didn't talk while we ate, but I felt relaxed and comfortable in our silence. Maybe I felt easy with him because I had no desire to impress him. He was a fine person, I was sure, but I had no wish to know him better. Dennis, however, was something else. If I could ever get over wanting Dave, I might give Irene some competition! Dennis was handsome, and he had a charm about him that would dazzle any woman. I hadn't expected him to be on the desk tonight, but I did wonder where he was. After Glenn and I had eaten and were finishing our drinks, I asked. "Where is everybody tonight?"

"Hmm—well, the President is in the White House—"

"Oh!" I waved my hand and laughed. "You know what I mean!"

"Okay. Candy and Debbie are bowling. Rick and Bret have gone home. Irene and Dennis went to Reno right after the dining room closed this afternoon—" I closed my eyes for a second. Any interest or expectation I might have had in this evening dissolved, and I felt drained and tired. After a moment or two I said, "I think I'll go on up to bed."

"You do look a little pale," he said with concern in his voice. "Don't worry about trying to work in the dining room tomorrow, because Debbie will stay a couple more days."

"How is—you know—what's her name?"

"Jean isn't doing very well. She had double pneumonia. Unfortunately she smokes and has a history of respiratory problems. Doc Davis said she'd be in the hospital another week, at best."

57

"I'm sorry for her—" I smiled faintly. "But the timing is good for me."

We were both silent for a moment. When I started to get up, Glenn put his hand on my arm. "Misty, what are you running from?"

His directness amazed me and caught me off guard. "Why do you ask that?" I tried to sound casual, but his penetrating gaze assured me he wasn't fooled. Should I tell him? I ached to talk about Dave, to pour out my heartache to someone, to hear someone offer words of sympathy. I guess what I really wanted was for someone to tell me how I could get Dave back. Glenn was a man. He could tell me what to do from a man's point of view. But Glenn was also going to be my employer for the next couple of weeks. Did I dare expose my heart to him? I took a deep breath and spoke softly. "Maybe I *am* running."

"You can tell me about it—if you want to."

I wanted to. I talked non-stop, except for one time when Glenn had to attend to the switchboard, and another time when someone needed his door key. I told him the whole sad story, from being in love and practically engaged to Dave, down to the telephone conversation with Sharon, and my escape from Reno.

"And so you gave up a job so you wouldn't have to face Dave?"

"Of course! How could I stand to face him, knowing he didn't love me anymore?"

"From what you've told me," Glenn said, picking up a pencil and turning it in his fingers, "you've done nothing to be ashamed of—so why should you run?"

I stared at him wide-eyed. He didn't understand! "But don't you see? It would hurt me too much to see him!"

"More than you're already hurting?" Glenn's voice was

calm, logical. "What you're doing is twisting the knife in your own heart. The best way to get over any hurt is to face it."

I picked up the malt container, looked in it, then crumpled it, and tossed it in the wastebasket. "Are you suggesting I go back to Reno?"

Glenn studied his nails and shrugged. "I can't say that. You've already given up your job, and we need you here. But—hindsight is always better. If you had it to do again, it would have been best to talk it over."

"But there's nothing to talk over! He wanted me to—to—" I bit my lower lip. "And Sharon was there—ready and willing."

"Misty—" His voice was low, and his manner earnest. "Misty, you can't fault a man for being a man. I'm sure you've heard the old cliché that the best of men are only men at their best."

My mouth dropped opened, and I felt anger rising. I glanced around the lobby to be sure we were alone. "Are you defending Dave?" I rasped.

"I'm only saying if you still love the man, you ought to be fair and—"

"Fair! For a whole month he tricked me! Was *he* being fair?"

"No, he wasn't. But he's human, and without God's help, one's baser instincts often take over. Your Dave is no worse than many men."

I lifted my chin and tossed my hair back over my shoulders. "Then I don't want him—or any man!" I stood up, but Glenn took my hand and tugged gently. Frowning, and with my mouth tense, I sat down again.

"Have you ever read the New Testament about the woman caught in adultery?" His face was close to mine and I could see copper-colored flecks in his green eyes. Although his eyebrows were light brown, his eyelashes were almost black.

"Yes, of course I have." I was ashamed of the tone in my voice, but somehow his pious attitude irritated me.

"Then you remember what Jesus said to the men who were ready to kill her—'he who is without sin let him cast the first stone.'"

I maintained a still silence. I couldn't understand his attitude at all. Wasn't he a kind of preacher? What standards did he have, anyway?

"Misty, do you feel that you live completely within God's law at all times?"

I sniffed impatiently. "Of course not. No one does."

"Yet you expected Dave to live sinlessly."

I didn't answer. There were so many emotions popping around inside me I felt I might lose all composure and scream. "Let's not talk about it anymore," I said. "I'm sorry I told you my troubles. They'll work out." I took a breath, squared my shoulders, and smiled politely. "Tell me about yourself. You said you had decided to become a preacher at a young people's meeting. How old were you?"

Glenn didn't look as though he were ready to change the subject, but he was polite enough to go along with me. He tipped his cola container and shook out the last piece of ice. He crunched it thoughtfully. "About thirteen or fourteen. Our church was really a going concern in those days, but the youth leaders have either died off or moved away, and things change." He smiled wistfully. "When I was in high school, I felt led to become a minister in our church. My mother encouraged me, but my dad was never too excited about having a preacher in the family. He wanted me to work with him here in the hotel." He shook his head and smiled wryly. "That was the last thing I wanted to do—but it looks as though old dad got his wish."

"What do you mean?" I asked, genuinely interested.

"After high school Mom used some money she had saved to send me to Bible college, and Dad didn't mind too much. He knew I should go to college, and as long as I worked summers here at the inn, he was satisfied." Glenn had to take a call on the switchboard, then he continued. "Mom died my last year of college, and somehow it softened Dad. He paid for one year of seminary, and then—just eight months ago—he died." He compressed his lips and looked down at his shoes. I had a strange compulsion to try to comfort him, but I didn't move. "So—everything was willed to me." He lifted his arms and made a sweeping gesture. "Including a list of debts you wouldn't believe." Suddenly he smiled. "The only thing I got that was free and clear was a Honda—and it's a beauty. Dad had good taste in cars."

"How come Dennis works here?" I blurted, without thinking.

"Now that's an interesting story." He raised one eyebrow slightly. "Dad always especially liked his sister— that's my Aunt Frances, and Dennis is her son, so Dad willed Dennis five thousand dollars—which didn't exist after funeral expenses. Dad didn't believe in insurance. Dennis, meanwhile, was working in Reno as a business manager in one of the clubs, and for reasons he has never told me, was looking for a change. He was disappointed when I couldn't pay him the money Dad left him, but I offered him a job managing this place. And I have to say, he's good. Every week things improve a little."

The front door opened and a gust of cold wind blew a few papers off the counter. Glenn and I both looked up, and I was filled with warm excitement.

"Speak of the—" Glenn began.

"Don't say it, cousin!" Dennis laughed, as he held the

61

door open for Irene. She was dressed in tight black pants, a black cashmere sweater, and high-heeled black boots. For the first time, I saw her with her auburn hair swinging loosely around her shoulders. She could have been a teenager. She was laughing until she saw me, and then her expression became masklike. I didn't let it bother me though, because when Dennis saw me, there was no denying the pleasure in his eyes.

CHAPTER 9

DENNIS BOUNDED ACROSS THE lobby and leaned over the counter, beaming at me. "Alice! Old Doc must be a miracle-worker!"

Glenn evidently noticed the way Dennis looked at me, too, because a puzzled expression rested briefly on his face.

Irene flipped her hair back and raised her eyebrows.

"Even Doc can heal somebody who isn't sick," she scoffed. She started to go into the bar, but I decided I couldn't let that remark pass. I stood up.

"Irene, wait a minute, please." She turned and looked at me with her hazel eyes as round and hard as marbles. "I know I've caused you, and everyone else, a lot of trouble," I said, "and I'm really sorry. But whether you believe it or not, I've been awfully sick!" My voice began to waver. "I'd like to get along with you, Irene, but I won't allow you to call me a liar!"

The lobby got mausoleum quiet, and it was as though we'd all been sprayed with instant statue solution. Glenn stared down at the switchboard and Dennis gawked at me.

Irene and I were locked in an ocular battle. She was the first to look away. She grated, "I didn't call you a liar." She lifted her chin and stalked into the bar.

As soon as she was out of sight, I began to cry. Glenn was by my side instantly and, as though I were a child, he hugged me to his chest. Over my head he hissed, "Dennis, can't you get Irene to control that tongue?"

"Yeah," he growled. "I could cut it out with one of her knives."

I gasped and looked up at Glenn. His expression was exactly like my father's when I was in the seventh grade, and he had caught my older cousin making fun of my braces. It gave me a warm feeling, and I rested against him a moment. Reluctantly I moved out of his arms. Dennis reached across the counter and touched my arm. "Alice," he said in a low voice, "if there was any way we could do without her, I'd fire her tonight. But her culinary skills are our bread and butter."

I shook my head, alarmed. "I wouldn't want you to do that! I just wish I could learn how to get along with her."

"Please don't let it get you down," Glenn said. "We need you, too."

"I especially need you, Alice!" Dennis said, taking my hand. "Are you well enough to go for a ride in my Mercedes?"

"No, she's not," Glenn interjected. "And her name is *Misty*. She was just getting ready to go up to bed when you came in."

Dennis looked at me. "That's right," I admitted. Even though I was attracted to Dennis, I didn't feel up to any more conversation. Anyway, if I ever had a date with him, I wanted to be dressed up and at my best. It was enough tonight just to know that he wanted to take me for a drive.

"Glenn," I touched his arm. "If you want to tell Debbie not to come in, I'm sure I'll feel like working tomorrow."

"No, I think you should have one more day to rest," he said, patting my shoulder.

"I agree!" Dennis winked at me. "I'll take you for a drive in the morning, okay?" He looked at Glenn. "Well? Wouldn't a nice drive around the countryside be therapeutic?"

Glenn frowned slightly, then shrugged as though he didn't care.

I told both men goodnight and went up to my room.

In my room I put on an old pair of pajamas, and sorted out my laundry. Since I was going to stay for a while longer, I would have to find a self-service laundry tomorrow. I rolled up my soiled clothes and put them in the tiny closet, then turned on the TV, found a movie that seemed interesting, and got into bed. Because I had slept a good part of the day, I was wide awake. I was sort of watching the movie, mulling over the remarks Glenn had made about Dave, and thinking about going for a drive with Dennis, when there was a knock at the door. It startled me. Who could it be? Candy? "I'll bet it is," I whispered and hurried to the door. "Who is it?" There was no answer. Was it Dennis? A wave of excitement went through me. If it was, I would never let him in at this hour—especially not in these old rags. "Who's there?"

"Me," a feminine voice answered.

I opened the door, smiling. "Candy—" But it wasn't Candy. It was Irene. She pushed past me.

"Close the door," she ordered.

I could smell liquor on her breath, and it made me apprehensive. My family didn't drink, and I wasn't comfortable with people who did. "Irene!" I whispered.

"Right." Her voice was taunting. "Who were you expecting? Dennis?"

"Who do you think you—"

"Who do you think *you* are, Miss Smart Aleck? You really made me look like a fool tonight!" Her eyes were so wild and her face so contorted I thought she might hit me, and I stepped back. I hated quarrels and scenes. What could I do? She was evidently drunk or she wouldn't be here. "I knew the first time I laid eyes on you, you'd be trouble. 'Alice-in-Wonderland,' my foot!"

"Irene, if you're worried about Dennis, forget it! I'm not the least bit interested in him—and even if I was, he's too old for me." I hoped she got the dig. "Besides, I have a boyfriend!" I felt the prick of conscience as I told these lies, but I had to get this crazy woman out of my room. "Now if you don't mind, I'd like to get some sleep tonight." I stepped toward the door. But she wasn't giving up that easily.

"Maybe you aren't interested in Dennis, but he's hot for you! I know him—and I'll clue you, babe, keep your hands off him. I didn't give up a good job in Reno and come to this rathole just to lose him!"

I lifted my chin in an effort to appear aloof and calm, but my heart was pounding. "Irene, I have no idea what you're talking about, but if you don't get out of my room right now I'll—"

She seized my wrist. "You'll what?" Frightened, I jerked away from her. "If you had any brains you'd leave," she said through clenched teeth. "But if you stay, get this through your dumb, blond head. I am your boss. And you'd better produce, because I'll be looking for any little excuse to have you fired." She gave me a little push as she went out. I quickly put the night lock on, then rested my head on the door.

Now what? How could I work under such conditions? "I've got to leave," I murmured. But the same problems I had before were still with me—I didn't want to go home, and I couldn't bear the thought of seeing Dave with Sharon in Reno. Besides, I needed the money I could earn here to pay what I owed Glenn and Dennis.

I was too tense to sleep, and I didn't feel like watching TV. Anyway, a sign on the door said all sets were to be turned off by eleven, and it was almost that time. Aimlessly I walked over to the dresser and opened the top drawer. I saw a Gideon Bible. I should have looked in there this afternoon when I wanted something to read, I thought. I picked it up. Still, I probably wouldn't have read it. I had had enough Bible reading and devotions when I was young. I wouldn't admit it to anyone, but the Bible bored me. It seemed to be mostly history, and I hated history. Yet I respected it, and mother had always said, "It's God's letter to us."

I opened it to the Psalms and read the first verse that caught my eye: "I call to the Lord, who is worthy of praise, and I am saved from my enemies." I drew in my breath, and a shiver went over me. I rubbed the gooseflesh on my arms. Irene was my enemy! If I called on the Lord, would He help? I could almost hear my mother say, "Oh, Misty! Of course He'd help." She had urged me to study the Bible and pray—daily devotions, she called it. "It's your strength, honey." The first couple of weeks in college I had tried to have devotions, but it was all I could do to keep up with the required reading, so I gave up on it.

But I did believe in God. I remembered the night I left Reno, after my close call with the truck, that I had sort of prayed—and He had answered! Hadn't He shown me that sign and brought me to a place where the people were kind to me? Except for Irene. I put the Bible back in the drawer, then got in bed and turned out the light. The sheets felt icy and I rubbed my feet together. I was just getting warm when I remembered I hadn't taken my medicine. I got up, struggled with the child-proof top on the container, then swallowed one of the large capsules. It may have had a sedative in it, because it wasn't long until I was sleepy. But just before I went to sleep I thought, *Lord, save me from my enemy*.

The next morning Irene's visit seemed almost like a dream. Her behavior had been so bizarre. Had the whole thing really happened? A small red place on my wrist assured me it had. While I took a shower I had several imaginary conversations with her—rehearsing both how to work out our problems and how to tell her off. One part of me wanted to run away again. I actually was a little bit afraid of her. But the Irish in me made me want to fight back. Why should I let her intimidate me? I would work here as long as it was convenient, and I would leave when I wanted to.

I dressed carefully in pink designer jeans and a pink-and-white striped top. I started to wear a comfortable pair of canvas ballerina shoes, but decided if Dennis did take me for a drive, I should wear high heels. I got my old stand-by sandals out of the suitcase. They still looked pretty good, but the cork on one heel was beginning to look shabby. I sighed. Whether I stayed here or went to Stockton, I was going to have to start earning some money. The old checking account was beginning to look shabby, too.

My hair turned out nicely after I curled it with the wand. I pinned it up on top of my head, with little wispy curls in front of my ears. I used a touch of eye-liner, and violet eye shadow. It helped to perk up my spirits. I felt well physically, but my ego, because of Dave, was still suffering. I put on brown mascara, then winked at myself. "Forget

Dave, Misty! There are plenty of fish in the sea—including Dennis.''

I wondered if Dennis really would take me for a drive this morning? Would he call? And if he did, would Glenn listen in? I took the bundle of dirty clothes out of the closet, then looked at my watch. It was already eight-thirty. I wasn't going to sit around this tiny room and wait for him to call. I'd go find a laundry some place and get that much done.

Glenn was at the desk talking on the phone when I got downstairs. He smiled and waved at me. I stood at the counter uncertainly for a moment. Should I ask Glenn if Dennis was around? I decided against that, and went out the door, across the veranda, and down the steps with my head high.

When I came out of the parking lot, I had no idea where to look for a self-service laundry. But I didn't have to drive around the little town of Donnerville very long before I saw a sign, "LAUNDROMAT.''

In an hour I was back at the inn, and Dennis was apparently watching for me. "I thought you had stood me up,'' he said as he held the door for me. He smiled and his dark eyes glowed when they looked into mine.

"Really?'' I glanced beyond him to see if Irene was anywhere around, but the only person I could see was Glenn, still busy on the switchboard. "How could I stand you up?'' I teased. "We didn't have a real date.''

"We did have a date,'' he insisted. "We're going for a drive, remember? Are you ready?''

"I didn't say I'd go, did I?'' I smiled up at him. He pretended to be angry and made a fist. "Okay, okay! But first, I have to put away these clothes.''

He looked at them. "Have you been shopping this early?''

"Oh, no!'' I laughed at his mistake. "It's laundry.''

69

"You went to a laundry? You didn't need to do that. We have a washroom here." He waved toward the back of the inn. "There's a utility room by the kitchen. Couple of washing machines, dryer, even a mangle. My aunt and uncle used to do all the linens, but we figure it's just about as cheap, and a lot easier, to send them out." As we started toward the stairway, he added, "You're welcome to use the stuff anytime—Candy and Irene do."

"Where is—where are they?"

He glanced in the empty dining room. "Must be back in the kitchen. They were here a minute ago." I sighed with relief. I knew I'd have to face that woman sometime, but I hoped it wouldn't be when Dennis was with me.

We went up to my room together, and he waited in the hall while I put away the clean clothes, came back out, and locked the door. He put his arm lightly around my waist and we began to hurry down, running the last few steps. We were both laughing when we reached the bottom.

Glenn looked up at us and smiled with his lips, but his eyes, which looked more gray than green this morning, were stern. Or was the expression sadness? "Hi, Misty," he said. "How are you this morning?"

"Wonderful!"

He studied my face a moment, then turned to Dennis. "That carpet man will be here at eleven. Will you and Misty be back by then?"

"Eleven!" Dennis mumbled something under his breath. "That's only an hour."

Glenn shrugged. "You told me to set up an appointment. I did."

Dennis's face looked ugly for a moment, but he brightened when he looked at me. "Well, an hour is better than nothing! Come on, Alice!" I waved at Glenn as Dennis pulled me out the door.

In his Mercedes, I spent the first few moments gazing at the interior. I had never been in such a luxurious car before, and I was impressed with how solid it looked and felt. Then I began to study Dennis's profile. My heart beat a little faster as I realized I was alone with this splendid-looking man. I also felt pangs of unfaithfulness. I had not been alone with any man since I broke up with Dave. And Dennis reminded me, heartbreakingly, of Dave.

"Have you ever heard of the Donner Party?" Dennis asked.

"Yes." I sat up a little straighter and turned toward him.

"I had planned to take you to see their memorial this morning, but now we won't have time."

"Oh, well, Dennis. That's okay." I leaned forward and grinned at him. "You can take me there sometime when we have a real date."

He laughed and put his hand over mine. "Have you had breakfast?"

"No," I said. "I—I wasn't especially hungry this morning."

He looked at me for a second, then back at the road. We were almost out of town, climbing on a narrow, state road toward the mountains. "Where are we going?"

"To eat breakfast." He didn't look at me as he shifted gears.

A shiver of anxiety went through me. Bret had said that besides the Royce Inn, there were only two other places in town to eat.

We rode along in silence for about two minutes. The only sound was the car's engine as it climbed. However, my heart was thumping so hard I was sure Dennis could hear it. Where was he taking me?

CHAPTER 10

THE SCENERY FROM THE car window was beautiful. The snow-capped Sierra Nevada mountains formed a backdrop for green hills, patches of wild flowers, blue skies, and billowy white clouds. Part of my mind marveled at the beauty of God's creation. And yet, I was too anxious to enjoy it.

Then, as we rounded a long curve, Dennis began to brake. On the left was a circle driveway, leading to a lovely, two-story, frame house. It was not quite a mansion, but it was very large, with a wide front porch and steps. The house was painted white, and all the shutters and "gingerbread" trim were green. It looked inviting, but as we got closer, I could see the house and grounds were showing signs of neglect. The shrubbery close to the front porch, which had evidently been trimmed to resemble animals in the past, now had shoots of new growth, making the "animals" appear as though they needed a haircut. Dennis stopped the car, jumped out, and hurried around to my side.

"Where are we?" I asked, as he helped me out. In spite

of the brilliant sunshine, an icy breeze came down from the mountains above us. I rubbed my bare arms and leaned slightly toward him.

"This is Mary Jo's," he said. He put my arm through his and covered my hand possessively. "She's the best cook I know."

"You'd better not let Irene hear you say that!" I gave him a knowing look.

"She won't." He looked down at me. "I told you to forget her." He let his lips brush my hair, and a thrill sparkled through me.

"I'd like to," I said. "But she's my boss."

As we walked up the steps, he said, "No, she's not. *I* am. And Glenn, of course," he added.

"Dennis, it's none of my business, but is Irene your girl?"

He let go of my hand and looked at me incredulously. "My girl?" He laughed harshly and twirled the old-fashioned doorbell. "What makes you ask that?"

"She says she is," I answered, but before he could confirm or deny it, there was a slight movement behind the lace curtain on the door, then it swung open. A sweet-faced older woman, with shining white hair knotted at the nape of her neck, greeted us.

"Dennis!" she exclaimed. Her blue eyes sparkled. She was dressed in jeans, a western shirt and cowboy boots. "And who is this sweet thing you have with you?"

"Mary Jo, this is Misty—and we're starving to death for breakfast. Can you rustle us up something?"

"Come in, come in! You know I can." She turned and we followed her trim form across a wide foyer and into the dining room. On the way I caught a glimpse of the living room—blue wall-to-wall carpeting, a baby grand piano, shining tables, and Tiffany lamps.

In the dining room, besides a long table in the center of the room, there were two smaller tables near windows overlooking a side yard. "Come sit here." She pulled out a chair for me. "You can watch the birds while you eat." Several varieties of birds were eating from a hanging feeder, while others hopped around on the ground or splashed about in a marble birdbath. Dennis sat opposite me.

"How've you been, Mary Jo?" he asked.

A trace of sorrow touched her features for an instant, then she smiled. "Just fine! Now, what would you like to eat? I have fresh eggs, of course—and ham or bacon . . . Or if you want pancakes, it'll only take a minute—"

"An egg and toast would be plenty for me," I said, smiling up at her. "Over easy."

"That's fine for me, too," Dennis said. "Maybe you'd better make it two eggs—and I'd like some ham—and about four pieces of toast, if it's your good homemade bread."

Mary Jo nodded. "It is. Now you two relax. I'll bring coffee."

While she was gone, Dennis spoke quickly. "Mary Jo's husband died a few months ago, and she had a choice of either selling out or going to work. Cooking is what she does best, so she has let people around here know this home is available for small dinner parties, or even lunch and breakfast."

"But isn't she competition for Royce Inn?"

He shrugged. "I suppose so. But she's so doggone nice, and I don't think she'll hurt us, because we're aiming for the tourist trade. Mary Jo wants to reach the local people. She said it would seem more like she was entertaining friends instead of making a living."

"Irene said the townspeople are Royce's main business, too."

"Only in our dining room. I'm working on some package deals with a few of the clubs in Reno, and making some contacts with travel agencies in both San Francisco and L.A." He smiled and winked. "I also know a few desk clerks who owe me favors. They've promised to recommend Royce Inn whenever they can."

Mary Jo brought coffee in a silver pot, and poured it steaming hot, into bone china cups. "I'll have your breakfast in a couple minutes," she promised, and disappeared again. I lifted my cup, and while it was too hot to sip, I inhaled the rich aroma.

"Most people want to stay in Reno, of course," Dennis continued, "but there are some who prefer to be in the mountains. Royce Inn has comfortable accommodations, including a gourmet dining room, and our rates are considerably lower than those in Reno." He bobbed his head for emphasis. "Besides that, we're close to several lakes, including Lake Tahoe, and there's plenty of good fishing in the area. In Donnerville there's horseback riding, bowling, miniature golf, and roller skating." He drew a breath and smiled wickedly. "If old Dad doesn't like to fish, he can get his family happily occupied, then slip away and be pulling handles in Reno in an hour."

I laughed and shook my head. "You're awful!"

"Just doing my job, lady."

"You seem to be enjoying it," I said.

"Hate it. I'd rather be pulling handles myself."

"Really? You seem much too intelligent to gamble."

"You're right." He drew a deep breath and twisted his fork back and forth on the linen cloth. "I don't do much gambling."

Mary Jo brought our breakfast then, and for the next several minutes, we enjoyed the taste of fresh eggs, homemade bread, and a second cup of coffee, all served graciously on expensive china. If this was a sample of her culinary skills, she was better than "Irate Irene"! Why, I thought to myself, couldn't *she* cook for the Royce Inn?

Dennis touched his lips with a snowy napkin, then looked at his watch. "I've got seven minutes to be back at the Inn." He stood up, took my hand, and pulled me to my feet. "Sorry, Mary Jo," he called out, "but we have to run."

She hurried out of the kitchen, drying her hands. "Oh, shoot! Do you have to go? I was hoping we could visit awhile."

"We'll be back," he promised, taking bills out of his wallet. He pressed them into her hand, and she tried to make him take some of them back. He gave her hand a firm squeeze, then kissed her cheek. "When we have more time, I want to talk over some business with you." We said our goodbyes, got in the Mercedes, and drove back to town.

Dennis parked in back of the hotel in a parking spot marked "Reserved," next to a silver Honda, which had to belong to Glenn. We crossed a charming, private yard, with a small patch of grass, some potted palms, blooming roses, and other flowering plants. To the left of the yard was a receiving dock, and an old-fashioned, screened back porch. "The porch leads to the laundry room I was telling you about," Dennis said. "Beyond that is the kitchen."

He guided me toward a sliding glass door at the right of the yard, unlocked it, and stepped aside so I could enter. I was relieved when I realized I wouldn't have to go through the kitchen and see Irene. As I passed through the opening, he touched my back with his hand. It felt large and hot through my thin shirt. He whispered, "Alice, you're really something."

As soon as my eyes got accustomed to the dimness, I could see we were in a living room, furnished with well-worn leather furniture. "This is where Glenn and I hang out in our spare time." He looked at his watch and swore. "I'd ask you to sit down, but I'm already seven minutes late." He grinned and snapped his fingers. "Hey! Why don't you come and help Glenn and me choose carpet? Three rooms upstairs have to be completely renovated."

"I'd love to!" I said with enthusiasm. Though I hated for the time with Dennis to end, I was very interested in interior decorating. I had taken a six-week course a few years ago, and at one time had thought I'd like to be an interior decorator. It had never worked out, though I loved selecting colors and fabrics and arranging furniture for aesthetics and efficiency.

The decorator was in the lobby with Glenn, discussing prices, availability, and labor, when Dennis and I walked in. Glenn seemed especially pleased to see me. We went upstairs and took a look at the three rooms. Both Glenn and Dennis encouraged me to speak up and express my opinions about what was needed in the way of drapes and wall coverings, as well as carpets. As if I were being guided, I seemed to know what would look the best in each room. The carpet man, whose name was Allen, remarked, "This young lady knows her stuff!" I felt a warm blush of pleasure steal up my neck and into my face, and as Dennis and Glenn beamed at me, I felt pretty and a little bit important.

It was almost two o'clock in the afternoon before Allen put away all his samples, shook hands all around, and left. Glenn and Dennis both seemed exhausted, and plopped down in the lobby—Dennis, on the couch and Glenn, in one of the big chairs. For some reason I felt exhilarated. I loved the feel of the drapery swatches, and all the carpeting was so beautiful. I couldn't wait to see what the rooms would look like, redecorated in my choices.

"When do you think he'll start work?" I asked.

Glenn looked at Dennis, and shrugged. "Possibly next week. Doubtful though. His company is one of the best in Reno, so he's in constant demand."

"Ah—that's too bad. I probably won't get to see the rooms when they're finished."

"Why?" Glenn said, sitting up straighter. "I thought you'd decided to stay on."

I smiled at him and shook my head. "You know I didn't say I'd stay . . . I mean, *forever*."

"Why don't you, Misty?" Dennis asked. "There's no real reason for you not to."

"Oh, sure!" I shook my head. "Even if I wanted to, how about Jean? She'll need her old job back when she gets well." The two men looked at each other. I couldn't tell what they were thinking, and they didn't speak. "I have to get a job! Even though I was making good money in Reno, I didn't have enough sense to save any." I compressed my lips and frowned. "My checking account is just about kaput." I sighed. "So, as much as I hate to go back to Stockton, I have no choice. Pretty soon, I won't even have enough money to buy a tank of gas."

Glenn cleared his throat and leaned forward slightly. "Dennis, would it be possible to fit another salary into the budget?"

Dennis raised an eyebrow. "What do you have in mind?"

"Well—Misty's right. We are honor bound to give Jean back her job when she's well, but you know how confining it is to be at the desk when both you and I have business elsewhere." Dennis shifted his position and barely nodded. Glenn continued as if I were not even there. "Also, I know it hasn't been easy for you to type all that correspondence to the travel agencies, and I'd like to be free from the book-keeping." He looked at me. "Misty was an administrative assistant in Reno. She can surely handle any of our office work—right, Misty?"

I shrugged and smiled. "I'm sure I'm better at office work than I am in the dining room."

"If Misty would consider minimum wage for just a month . . ."

Dennis shook his head. "Glenn, we can't ask Misty to do that. Anyway, we're barely meeting our utility bills. We haven't had enough overnight guests this past week to pay for the ads I've put in the brochures in Reno."

The lobby was quiet while each of us pondered our own thoughts. Last night Glenn had advised me to face my problems. Maybe I should return to Reno and try to get my job back. But I didn't want to go to Reno. And I had no desire to spend a long, hot summer in Stockton. I wanted to stay right here, in these beautiful mountains, in a picturesque town, with my friends, Candy and Glenn—and Dennis. I looked at him now, hunched forward, with a worried look on his face.

"Don't feel bad, Dennis," I said, smiling. "I'll work until Jean comes back, and by that time we'll know what to do, I'm sure! Everything always works out."

He smiled. "I've been thinking—I don't know if you'd go for it or not." He looked at Glenn and then back at me. "Would you consider . . ." He bit his lip and frowned. "It's nervy of me to ask you, but would you consider working for your room and board? Just until we start getting some of the tourist trade?"

Glenn brightened. "Hey, now that's a thought! July and August have always been good months—even without any package deals." The switchboard buzzed and Glenn stood up and started toward the desk. "What do you say, Misty?"

Dennis stared up at me from under heavy, dark eyebrows. Every time I allowed myself to look directly into his eyes, my stomach dropped as though I were riding an elevator. I looked away quickly and tried to be rational. At Sorensen Engineering I had not only made a good salary for a woman my age, but I had enjoyed a certain amount of prestige. If I took this job I would be a desk clerk—and for no pay! It was so ridiculous I almost laughed. Instead I whirled around to face Glenn and, as he picked up the headset, I called over to him, "Okay, Glenn! I'll stay."

Dennis jumped up and put his arm around my waist and squeezed me. "Alice! That's great! You won't regret it." He looked around the lobby with a special light in his eyes. "This place is going to be booming!" He winked at me. "You'll be on salary before you know it. I promise you!" He took my hand and swung it back and forth. "And when you need gas for that little Camaro, you simply use our credit card."

"Oh, no!" I protested. "I won't let you buy my gas!"

"Why not? You'll become a necessary expense and a beautiful deduction."

"That's right, Misty," Glenn added. I turned to look at him. He was nodding his head and smiling rakishly. "You're the prettiest deduction we've ever had!" Both men laughed and exchanged a look. Glenn added, "If you're willing to work for us without pay for a little while, the least we can do is take care of your expenses."

"Come on," Dennis said, and pulled me toward the dining room. "Let's get some of Irene's lunch specials before she puts everything away."

My happiness faded. For a little while I had forgotten her.

CHAPTER 11

I DREADED SEEING IRENE, and yet I knew I couldn't postpone it forever. With my feet almost dragging, I went with Dennis into the dining room. Candy and Debbie were seated at a table near the entrance eating a late lunch. When Candy saw us come in, she waved her fork and grinned. "Hi, y'all! Hey, Misty, where you been? I came to see you this morning and you had flew 'de coop. I thought you were supposed to be sick."

"I was sick, believe me! But, thanks to antibiotics and clean living, I'm fine today."

Debbie laughed and shook her mass of auburn curls. "That means you'll be back on the job tomorrow, right?"

Before I could answer, Dennis cut in. "Deb, could your aunt get along without you for a few more days? Glenn and I want to teach Misty the switchboard, and also some of the office work."

Debbie shrugged. "She probably wouldn't mind. Our shop isn't doing too much business yet, 'cause there haven't been that many tourists. I can ask her."

"Would you? We'd like to start Misty in the office in the morning."

"As soon as I finish here, Dennis, I'll go ask her."

"Ask who what?" I jumped when I heard Irene's voice. She had come up beside us so quietly that none of us had noticed her.

Dennis frowned slightly. "I've just asked Debbie to work a few more days, until Jean gets well."

"Why? Is Miss Alice-in-Wonderland still sick?" She seemed to be joking, and there was a smile on her face. "You look like you feel wonderful!" She patted my shoulder as if I were a favorite! I could not understand her at all. I searched her eyes for a long moment. Was there any message there? She seemed friendly enough, but what about last night? Was it possible she had been so drunk that she didn't remember? No. She hadn't staggered, or been thick-tongued. What was she trying to pull? With a concerned look, she asked. "Are you going home?"

Her question startled me. What should I say? Dennis answered for me.

"No, Irene. Misty has agreed to work for us as a—if you'll pardon the expression, Misty—as sort of a Girl Friday. She'll be on the switchboard, and doing some of the office work."

Irene's pleasant expression changed. As a stretched piece of old rubber gradually regains its shape, her usual mask of hostility fell into place. "How strange!" she said to Dennis. "You didn't mind offering me half my former salary in Reno—and I've worked hard for you for six months without a raise. Couldn't afford it, you said! But these girls come along, and suddenly you can afford all kinds of help!" Her eyes widened as she glared at him, and thrust out her chin defiantly. Then she whirled around to leave, but Dennis caught her arm.

82

"Irene!" His voice was guttural. "Misty is going to work for room and board until our income picks up—at which time, if you're still with us, you will receive a substantial raise."

Out of the corner of my eye, I saw Debbie move quickly across the lobby and out the front door. Irene's neck reddened and her mouth became a straight, red line. She looked at me with cold hatred, then walked out into the lobby.

As soon as she was out of sight, Dennis pulled out a chair for me and we sat down at the table with Candy. He spoke cheerfully, as though he had already dismissed the unpleasant incident. "Candy, when you finish your lunch, could you bring us something to eat?"

"You mean 'Days of Our Lives' is all over?" She chuckled. She stood up and picked up the lunch dishes on the table. "Sure, Mr. Parker. The sirloin tips were excellent."

While she was in the kitchen, I said, "Dennis, I really want to work here. But, honestly, I don't think I can take any more of Irene's sarcasm. I don't know—"

Dennis put his hand over mine. "I apologize for her, Misty. I've known her for years, and she's always had a sharp tongue, but the last few days she's been unbearable. I don't know what her problem is."

"I know." I looked at Dennis and wondered if I should tell him about last night's visit. Would honesty be the best policy, or would it cause even more trouble? Before I had made a rational decision, I blurted, "Irene came to my room last night."

Dennis stiffened slightly. "And?"

"She told me to keep my hands off you."

He closed his eyes and turned away slightly. "I don't believe it," he said under his breath. Then, turning to me, he raised his voice a notch. "Yes, I *can* believe it. At the risk of sounding conceited, she's been after me for years."

"She told me she gave up a good job to follow you. Well, I heard her say practically the same thing a few minutes ago. Is that true?"

He nodded. "She was in charge of the waitresses at the Seventy-Seven Club. Ever been there?"

I shook my head. "I don't gamble."

"I'll have to teach you sometime." He gave my hand a squeeze. "Anyway, she was making a lot of money, with tips, and . . ." He paused and pursed his lips. "But she wasn't happy there. She had some problems." He sighed and frowned, as though it irritated him to remember. "She had a fit when I told her I was going to come here, and she jumped at the chance to get away from Reno when I asked her if she wanted to work here as our chef. Why shouldn't I use her skills? But I didn't force her to come."

Use her skills? Somehow, the word *use* jarred me. No matter what I thought of Irene, the idea of Dennis using her seemed unfair. I wondered if he would use anyone who was willing and available? But I dismissed these thoughts. He was so good-looking, pleasant, funny, delightful to be with! He had helped so much to ease the pain over Dave. Hah! Who was Dave, anyway? I smiled warmly and Dennis hugged my shoulder. "I'm glad to see you smile, little Alice! I think we have a great summer ahead of us. And, to start it off, how would you like to have a real date with me tonight?"

"Like what?" I flirted.

"Like dressing up, and going in to Reno to a private, exclusive club, where we'll dine on filet mignon and lobster, and dance to the music of a real orchestra."

"Oh, that would be exciting. But there *is* one thing. I don't know how to dance."

He pulled away to look at me in surprise. "You're kidding!"

I shook my head. "No, it's true. My parents said dancing was a tool of Satan's, so I never learned."

Dennis laughed. "But surely in college . . ."

"I've been practically engaged ever since college days and Dave—my boyfriend—didn't know how to dance, either."

"Engaged? He took my left hand, and his finger traced the white circle on my third finger. "So, that's why you left Reno."

I looked away for a moment. "But it's all over now!" I tossed my head defiantly, and some of my curls came loose. Dennis chuckled and tried to help me pin them back in place.

"It's okay," I said, and took out all the hairpins, letting my hair tumble down around my shoulders. Dennis played with the strands, then rested his hand on the back of my neck. The expression on his face was tender, and our eyes met for a breathtaking moment.

Candy brought our lunch then. As I turned in my chair, I could see Glenn leaning against the counter. He seemed to be staring at me but, without my glasses on, I couldn't really see his expression. "Glenn hasn't had any lunch either!" I exclaimed.

"I know. As soon as we eat, I'll take over, and you can stay with me. I'll teach you how to listen in on calls." He winked.

"Dennis! Shame on you! Listen, how can we go out tonight? You're supposed to work at the desk?"

"We won't leave until after ten o'clock. Nothing ever happens after that—and if it does, the night bell rings by Glenn's bed."

"Ten o'clock! I'm supposed to work tomorrow."

"Not to worry." He leaned back so Candy could place the steaming plate before him. "Remember, I'm the boss."

"Yeah! Remember, he's the boss!" Candy echoed. I smiled at her, but instead of easing my mind, I couldn't help worrying about how I would feel the next day. I had always been a morning person, functioning best from five A.M. until about twelve or one. I liked to go to bed early. Besides, I certainly didn't want to have a relapse of the virus. I also felt sorry for Glenn. He was the owner of the inn, and yet it seemed to me that Dennis was in control. Although the sirloin tips looked delicious, I didn't feel very hungry. I kept hoping Dennis would get through so we could relieve Glenn. I glanced at the desk again, and found him still looking at me.

After Dennis and I finished eating, we went to the desk together. "Ready to have some lunch, Cuz?" Dennis asked.

"I'm not too hungry," Glenn answered.

"You don't look as though you feel very well," I said.

"Maybe I'm coming down with Misty's bug." He grinned slightly.

"Oh, no!" I bit my lip. "I knew that would happen! I wonder how many others I've infected?"

"Don't worry," Glenn said. "You had no way of knowing. You didn't do it on purpose. Anyway, I'm probably just tired. A good night's sleep will take care of it."

"Speaking of sleep, Glenn. Would you mind too much being on call tonight?" Dennis smiled at me. "Misty and I are going over to Reno tonight for dinner."

"Dinner?" Glenn looked bleak.

"A late dinner. We probably won't leave here until ten."

"Oh." He nodded vaguely. "Sure. Sure, it's okay." He swallowed as though his throat hurt. "In fact, if you want to go earlier, I'll take care of things. Might be better. I mean, you'd get home earlier. We all have to work tomorrow."

"Okay!" Dennis accepted quickly and looked at me. "How about leaving around eight?"

I shrugged. "Whatever is best." I wasn't too eager to go, not only because of the late hours, but because it didn't seem quite fair to Glenn. Also, I had to admit, I had some kind of a hang-up about going to night clubs. And yet, why not? Who was to keep me from taking all I could from life? Wasn't that what Dave had done? The thought of him filled me with sadness for an instant. I looked up and smiled boldly. "What should I wear?"

"With your figure, baby, nobody's going to notice what you have on."

Glenn walked around the end of the desk and without a word, went into the dining room.

That afternoon Dennis taught me how to operate the switchboard. The hardest thing about it was learning not to disconnect callers when several calls were coming in at the same time. "As soon as we get a little cash built up, we'll go for a whole new system," he said.

"I enjoyed it," I said, "except when I disconnected room Fourteen."

Glenn must have come out of the dining room while I was concentrating on the switchboard, because I didn't see him any more that afternoon. About six o'clock, Dennis suggested I go take my shower and get ready; then, at seven or seven-thirty, I could take his place at the desk while *he* got dressed.

After showering I put on my most sophisticated dress. It was made of a soft, silky material—a beautiful shade of lavender—with a full skirt, dolman sleeves, and a low neck. I didn't have an appropriate wrap, so I picked up my black sweater and purse, locked the room, and went downstairs. Dennis whistled when he saw me, then left to take his shower.

I felt a little nervous sitting at the desk alone, but aside from two calls asking about the dinner special, the switchboard was quiet. It was interesting to watch people come in for dinner. A few drifted into the bar and, although I had never thought about it before, I wondered who was serving them? I crossed over the few steps and peeked around the corner. There was a door between the bar and the kitchen, and Irene was laughing and mixing drinks for a foursome. How could she be everywhere at once? She really was a wonder-worker. As I scooted back to the desk, I breathed a deep sigh. I was so glad I wouldn't have to work directly with Irene. She probably would have made me learn how to mix drinks.

"Hi, Misty." I whirled around to see Glenn. He didn't look well at all. He eyed me from head to toe. "Marvelous."

"Glenn—you *are* sick, aren't you?"

"Not feeling super, but I'm okay."

"I'll tell Dennis we mustn't leave—"

"No, no, I'm fine. You go ahead and enjoy yourself." He came around the end of the counter and stood next to me. His green eyes were dull, and his face looked dry. "But, Misty, be careful, okay?" He touched my arm, and his hand was hot. "Dennis is my cousin and I think a lot of him, but he runs in a fast crowd." He looked straight at me. "Just remember, you don't have to do everything they do."

I smiled at him. "Okay, Daddy." I squeezed his hand, then touched his forehead. "You feel so hot! You better take some of my antibiotics." Before he could protest, I ran up the stairs, unlocked my room, got the medicine, and hurried back down. "I guess I better take one more, too," I said. I went to the dining room and got each of us a glass of water. We "toasted" each other as we swallowed the huge capsules.

Glenn looked into my eyes. "You're a sweet girl, Misty."

"You've discovered that, too?" Dennis said, as he came from their living quarters. I saw Glenn look down quickly, as though he'd been caught stealing cookies. When I turned to look at Dennis, I had to suppress a gasp. He was so handsome! He was wearing a light blue suit with a vest, a white shirt, and blue tie. In my mind I compared Dennis with Dave. Dave was as handsome as Dennis, but he never wore a suit. His ski jackets and sports clothes were probably as expensive as suits, but he just didn't like to dress up.

"Well, Misty, are you ready to take on the biggest little city in the world?"

"Glenn is really not feeling well enough to be on the desk," I said.

Dennis looked at him impatiently.

"I'm all right," Glenn said. "You two have a good time." He turned away and began to leaf through the mail.

"Well," Dennis said to me. "You heard the man—let's go!"

In the Mercedes he put his arm around me and kept it there all the way to Reno. The bright lights of the casinos blinked and sparkled, stabbing the darkness with commands to stop and play. We drove past them, and finally wheeled into the underground parking lot of a tall building. We took an elevator to the fourteenth floor, and, when the doors opened, we walked out into the most opulent restaurant I'd ever seen.

The floor was covered with thick, red carpeting, and everywhere I looked were large, round tables, covered with white damask cloths that reached the floor. On every table were red roses—not just a single bud in a vase, but at least a dozen, long-stemmed beauties. There seemed to be an army of tuxedo-clad waiters, each carrying white towels over their arms. An orchestra was playing softly. The women seated at the tables looked beautiful and refined, and the men, like Dennis, wore suits. I felt self-conscious and wished I'd left my sweater in the car. The maitre d' knew Dennis, and greeted him with a big smile. "Ah, Mr. Parker—you would like to have your favorite table?"

"Later, Robert. Right now the lady and I would like to see some action."

CHAPTER 12

DENNIS GUIDED ME GENTLY along one wall until we came to a velvet-draped archway. I was becoming more apprehensive every moment. I had lived in Reno long enough to realize that "seeing some action" meant more than just pulling a few slot machine handles, and the thought of mingling with "big-time" gamblers frightened me. Dennis held the curtain aside, and I stepped into a large, red-carpeted gambling room. The room was glittering with the reflected light of huge mirrors and ornate crystal chandeliers. The place was crowded, and in spite of air conditioning, the cigarette smoke choked me. I was not only ill-at-ease, but I was puzzled, too. Financially, Dennis and Glenn seemed to have their backs against a wall. How could Dennis afford to come to a place like this, much less risk losing a lot of money? He stood still for a moment, resplendent in his blue suit, surveying the room. One of the dealers nodded at him, then gave me a sensual look.

"What are you going to do?" I whispered.

"I told you I was going to teach you how to gamble." He

winked at me. He seemed excited and looked so young and innocent that he could have been a teen-ager telling me he was going to teach me how to play a new computer game.

"Oh, Dennis, I don't want to be a spoil-sport, but I don't *want* to learn to gamble."

He put his arm around me and pulled me close. "Why?"

"Why?" I raised an eyebrow and wrinkled my nose. "It's dumb! People always lose."

"Not always," he said, looking over the room again. There were a couple of crap tables, a roulette wheel, blackjack and other card tables. The well-dressed people playing the games seemed to be serious and intense. There were also slot machines along one wall, and although some were being used, the room had an air of quiet dignity not found in the public casinos with their hundreds of machines whirring and clinking continuously.

Even Dave had scoffed. "There has to be something wrong with people who work hard all week, then throw away their wages on Saturday night." I had agreed with him. Also, I had been brought up to believe that, like dancing, gambling was wrong.

"Dennis, you said you didn't like to gamble," I pleaded.

As though he hadn't heard, he took my arm and we started across the room to a table where a man was just standing up, apparently ready to leave. I tried to feel calm and mature. After all, I was of age—whose business was it, anyway? But my heart was thudding. I pulled back and he turned to look at me.

"What's the matter?" he asked.

"Dennis, please, could we have dinner first?"

His eyes looked too bright. "Dinner?" he answered, but he was giving me only part of his attention. "Are you hungry?" His interest was on the game table where there was now an empty chair.

"Yes! I'm really hungry."

He looked down at me and, for a fleeting instant, a dark expression touched his features. Then, with a deep breath, he turned me around and we walked toward the archway. "Dinner it is," he said, with an attempt at cheerfulness.

When we were seated at "Mr. Parker's favorite table," which was beside the small dance floor, we were immediately surrounded by waiters. One poured ice water in stemmed crystal goblets; one placed a silver tray of appetizers on the table; another, with a flourish, handed us red-and-gold menus. They were in French, and I didn't have a clue as to what to order. I looked up at Dennis and caught him frowning.

"Dennis—you're upset with me, aren't you?"

"Upset?" He shrugged and smiled. "Of course not. Are you ready to order? Or do you want me to order for you?"

"Oh, please do," I said, giving him my best smile.

During this little exchange, I was flustered to discover a waiter had been standing right behind me. He now stepped forward with pen poised, ready to take instructions. With finesse, Dennis gave him our order. His French sounded marvelous—and romantic.

"Such savoir-faire!" I said sincerely, hoping to break through the invisible wall that had risen between us. He smiled briefly, then looked away. Both of us turned our attention to the orchestra and the couples on the floor. After a moment or two, I couldn't stand the silence. "Dennis! I know you're angry about not playing cards."

He looked at me politely. "Please, Misty, don't give it another thought."

"But it's ruined our fun!" I cried. "I'm a direct person, Dennis, and I'm sorry if I've spoiled your evening. But I want to tell you how I felt in that other room." He shrugged, and I continued. "It isn't that I think I'm better or

93

smarter than any of those people, but I feel out of place in that atmosphere."

He raised his eyebrows. "Fine," he said. "You're not in there. Let's forget it. Ah, here's the wine."

Pompously the waiter opened the green bottle and poured a small amount for Dennis, which he tasted. He gave a nod of approval, and the waiter poured a glass for me, then filled Dennis's glass. When the waiter was out of sight, I gave Dennis my glass of wine. He looked puzzled, then smiled, this time a genuine smile.

"Hey, Alice, are you for real? You don't smoke, gamble, dance, or drink!" He began to laugh, and I joined him. "You're just a sweet, little girl playing grown-up!" Even if Dennis was laughing at me, I was glad the tension was broken.

Two waiters served our meal. First came vichyssoise, a potato and onion soup. I was shocked, when I first tasted it, to discover that it was ice-cold. But it was delicious! Next was a warm salad made with several vegetables, including huge slices of mushrooms, all sautéed, and served with a hot dressing. The waiters hovered nearby, ready to add a drop of water to already full glasses, pouring Dennis more wine, and snatching away dishes as soon as we put down our silverware.

"Good service is one thing," I whispered to Dennis, "but these fellows are giving me claustrophobia!" He chuckled and nodded. It was wonderful to see him in good spirits again. "What did you order for me?" I asked.

"Cotelette d'agneau," he answered, then laughed at my puzzled look. "Lamb, my lamb. Lamp chops. They're absolutely succulent!" I shuddered inwardly. My mother never served lamb because Daddy said mutton wasn't fit to eat. As far as I knew, I'd never tasted it, and didn't want to. I started to remind Dennis that he'd promised me steak and lobster, but I decided I had upset him enough for one evening. At least he hadn't ordered snails.

"You know," he went on, "everything served here is absolutely fresh, cooked after it's ordered. They're cooking our lamb right now." He sipped his wine, and I noticed the glass I had given him was also empty. I hoped he wouldn't drink too much, and I was glad when the waiters arrived with the rest of our meal.

The lamb chops were a delicate pink, and tastefully arranged on hot platters, garnished with thinly sliced potatoes, parsley, and mushrooms. The waiter offered us three kinds of bread, all fresh and hot. Although I hadn't expected to like the lamb, I ate almost all of it.

"Good girl," Dennis said, and reached across the table to pat my hand. It was the first loving gesture he had made since we came from the gambling room.

"Oh, no!" I whispered when the waiter placed a dish before each of us which contained at least three kinds of sliced cheese and fresh pears. "I won't have room for dessert," I moaned.

"Oh, you have to have dessert!" Dennis insisted. "It's white chocolate ice cream covered with fresh raspberry sauce. I'll bet you've never tasted anything like it."

I could eat only a bite or two of the marvelous concoction, and was uncomfortably full when I excused myself to go to the powder room.

Like everything else in the club, the ladies' room was exquisite. There was a royal blue carpet on the floor, and the furniture was Louis XIV. The walls were done in gold-and-white striped paper and adorned with large gilt-framed mirrors.

A young Mexican woman, dressed in a maid's uniform, handed me a linen towel when I washed my hands. I didn't know if I was supposed to pay for it, give her a tip, or accept it haughtily as my due. As I bit my lip in indecision, she motioned toward a porcelain tureen, holding a few dollar bills. She raised her eyebrows significantly, then turned and sat down in one of the fragile-looking chairs. I put a dollar in the bowl just as a glamorous woman about my age breezed in. Her long, wavy hair was a shade paler than mine. Her electric blue eyes were outlined in black, and the lids shaded in metallic brown and lavender. She wore a heavy layer of rouge and lipstick and a black dress which revealed her show-girl figure.

"Hi!" she said in a friendly voice. "I'm Sam, the cashier. I noticed you were with Dennis."

"Oh?" Who was this—another Irene? I felt the heat of jealousy creeping up in my face.

"I started to come over to your table earlier, but I got too busy—and now I guess he's in the little boys' room."

"Is Dennis a friend of yours?"

"Oh, sure. He's everybody's friend. He used to be the manager here."

"Really?" I felt a curious mixture of relief and bewilderment. Why hadn't he told me? "I didn't know."

"Whoops!" Sam clamped a hand over her mouth. "Maybe he didn't want you to know since he had some trouble—"

"En boca cerrada no entran moscas," the maid interrupted.

We both looked at her. "What did you say, Angela?" Sam asked.

"I just said, 'Flies can't get in a closed mouth.'" She gave Sam a knowing look, and the room was quiet.

I picked up my purse and sweater. "Glad to meet you Sam," I said. "I'd better go. I'll tell Dennis you want to see him."

"Right!" She waved as I went out the door.

Dennis was waiting for me near the ladies' room, and I told him about Sam. He took my arm, and we walked toward the elevator. "Aren't you going to wait until she comes out?" I asked. He shook his head, propelled me into the car, and pushed the Main Floor button. As the elevator descended he took me in his arms and kissed me, gently at first, then urgently. Feelings I had kept in check with Dave were suddenly unlocked, and I put my arms around his neck and pressed my lips against his. When the door opened we were both breathless. I smiled self-consciously at the people waiting to enter, certain they knew we had been kissing. In the parking area we walked along with our arms around each other. Oh, how I wished Dave could see me now! In the car I looked over at Dennis. He was so mature and sophisticated. I wondered how I could have been so heartbroken over Dave, less than a week ago! Probably my guardian angel was trying to get me to slow down but, if he was, I ignored him, and snuggled closer to Dennis.

When we were almost to the Royce Inn, Dennis drove down into a little gully and turned off the key. He faced me and, by the light of the full moon, I could see his eyes— beautiful, deep, thrilling. He pulled me close and kissed me. I responded to his soft lips, and he whispered, "Little Alice . . ." He began to stroke my back and arms lightly. It was wonderful to be loved again. But when his hand touched my thigh, I stiffened. "Dennis!" I looked at him, wide-eyed.

He put his mouth over mine. For the first time, I noticed the sour odor of liquor on his breath. I pulled away and moved toward my side of the seat.

"What's the matter?" he said, still trying to touch my leg. "Don't tell me you don't like this." He pulled me roughly over to his side of the car and forced his lips on mine. At the same time he began to pull at my dress. I pushed against his chest with both hands and broke free. "Dennis! I'm not like that!"

He stared at me, looking confused and angry. He ran his fingers through his hair and straightened his tie. "Talk about your dry runs," he muttered. Then he started the engine and pulled up onto the highway.

We stopped in front of the inn and Dennis got out and opened my door. Courteously he helped me up the steps and opened the front door. Glenn turned to look at us.

"You don't mind going up to your room alone, do you?" Dennis asked.

"Aren't you coming in?" I asked.

"Not now." The pupils of his eyes were large and dark. "But I'm sure it's time for little girls to go night-night," he said, with a trace of sarcasm.

I watched him skip down the steps, get in the car and roar away. My shoulders slumped and my throat ached with unshed tears. I stood at the door and watched the tail lights disappear in the darkness, then I turned slowly and crossed the lobby to the desk.

"You two have a spat?" Glenn spoke in a low tone.

I blinked back tears and walked around the counter. I plopped ungracefully in the steno chair and dropped my purse and sweater on the floor. At that moment Irene came out of the bar. Her long hair was down and looked disheveled. There were smudges of mascara on her cheeks, and her lipstick was gone. At first she didn't see me and addressed Glenn. "Did I hear Dennis? Wasn't that his car that just left?" I wished I could hide, but I sat there looking down at my feet.

"Yes," Glenn answered. "Dennis was here for a moment, but he took off again."

Then Irene saw me. "Well, did you finally get back? And how was your date to the big city?" She staggered slightly

98

as she walked toward the desk. She leaned on the counter and looked down at me. Her eyes were bloodshot and there was a looseness about her whole being.

"Fine," I answered, hoping she wouldn't ask any more questions.

"Let me tell you what you did," she said, and looked up at the ceiling, holding up her fingers as though counting. "First, you went to the club, that exclusive, indoor gold palace, and Dennis lost his shirt at poker." She shook her head and almost lost her balance. "I can't believe that he's such a fool he would keep putting money into a place that fired him."

I looked over at Glenn in time to see him lift his eyebrows slightly.

"I've tried to tell him. Lord knows I've tried." There was a little catch in her voice and her eyes filled with tears.

Glenn glanced at me, then touched Irene's hand. "You've had a hard day, Irene. Why don't you call it a night?"

She brushed her tears away. "I didn't finish telling Miss Smarty-Pants what she did tonight. You know, I can read minds!" She sniffed, then took a tissue from her blouse pocket and blew her nose. When she had her hair up and her make-up on, she was a beautiful woman. Tonight, she looked awful. "Then," she waggled her finger at me, "you ate a lot of French goop that's supposed to turn you on for the necking session, right?"

Glenn walked around the end of the desk and took Irene's arm. "Come on, Irene, let's get ready for another day."

Like a tired child she let him help her up the stairs.

I was ready to go upstairs, too. I was disillusioned, depressed, and exhausted. I hoped I could go right to sleep. The switchboard buzzed and I got up to answer it. After I made the connection, I sat down to wait.

When Glenn came back, he gave me a weak smile. He put his hands on my shoulders as he passed by. "Glad you're home," he said. He sat down on the stool and looked at me. "I tried not to worry—but, well, I guess you know a little bit about Dennis now." He looked sick, and his eyebrows were drawn together in a sorrowful expression. Yet his eyes glowed with compassion for me.

Against my will, I began to cry. "Oh Glenn, it was just awful!"

I leaned toward him and he moved forward so he could put his arms around me. He let me cry until I got control of myself. I reached inside the desk for a tissue, but he took it out of my hand, blotting the tears from my cheeks.

As I looked up at him, he kissed me on the forehead, and I closed my eyes. I felt his lips move down my face and touch mine very gently.

CHAPTER 13

ALTHOUGH I WAS GLAD to see Glenn feeling so much better the next morning, I dreaded to see Dennis. I felt degraded because of his behavior, and ashamed of my own.

I remembered Glenn's remark the night we were talking about Dave. He had said that the best of men are only men. So what could I expect from Dennis after falling all over him? What would I say to him? Should I apologize for leading him on? Or should I wait for him to say he was sorry? If only I never had to face him again!

I needn't have worried, because he didn't come back to the inn until sometime the next afternoon, and then he went right to bed. In fact, I didn't see much of Dennis for the next few weeks. He was always in Los Angeles or San Francisco on business and, when he came back, both he and Glenn were occupied with outside work. There was never a time when we were alone.

One of their outside projects was the reconditioning of the swimming pool, which hadn't been used for a couple of years. The two men were doing all the cleaning, scraping, and waterproofing themselves. The three of us—Glenn, Dennis, and I—established a routine. Glenn opened the desk early in the morning and sat at the switchboard until I came on duty at nine. Except for very short breaks, I worked until six in the evening when Dennis took over. My job included signing in guests, taking their money or filling out credit card vouchers, and showing them to their rooms if Candy or one of the boys wasn't available. Sometimes I thought I must be the biggest sucker in the world to work such long hours with no pay! But every time I analyzed my situation, I always concluded that this was best for now.

"I don't know what you would have done about this desk if I hadn't happened along!" I wisecracked one day as Glenn hurried by. He was dressed in dirty coveralls and carried a box of tools.

"Me, either," he answered. "But we'd have thought of something!" He winked and went out the front door.

The swimming pool area was to the left of the inn, and the bushes around it had grown so big that it could no longer be seen from the highway. Grass and weeds had also crept over the concrete deck. Cottonwood trees towered over the pool, dropping their leaves and fluffy cotton balls.

"Even after we get the pool ready," Glenn told me, "it can't be filled until we get those trees and bushes trimmed back."

That first couple of weeks at the switchboard was both frustrating and fun. I taught Candy how to answer calls so she could take over for a few minutes when I had to leave. She also brought me lunch every day, and when the dining room rush hours were over, she usually sat and talked to me for a while. Sometimes Debbie would come behind the desk, too, and we'd drink Cokes and talk about men. Occasionally Irene looked over at us with that cold and beautiful stare. But, as the days went by and she could see that

Dennis and I were not spending any time together, she thawed slightly.

Candy and I enjoyed each other. We laughed at the same dumb jokes, but we also covered more serious topics. For example, through our gabfests, I knew she had a boyfriend in Los Angeles and that she had lived with him for two years. "I want to get married, but he doesn't," she told me. "That's why I took this job." She grinned wickedly. "I gotta teach that dude a lesson."

Debbie told us she was crazy about a man in Reno, but he only called her once in a while. "It makes me wonder if he's married," she sighed. "And there's just nobody around here to date—unless you count Bret or Rick!" She also told us of her dream to go to Hollywood and become an actress.

I told them all about Dave, but I didn't tell them how deeply I felt about Dennis. Somehow, it seemed cheap and flighty that I could fall in love with another man so quickly.

Anyway, now I wasn't sure how I felt about Dennis. When he took over the desk in the evenings, he was always nice to me. He seemed exactly as he had before we'd gone to Reno. He never mentioned that tumultuous evening, and neither did I. It was as though he'd never touched me. We were co-workers and that was all. Sadly, I realized he didn't call me Alice anymore. But, philosophically, I believed that fate had let me meet Dennis to get over Dave. And now, maybe I was over both of them.

I told Glenn how I felt one morning as we had breakfast together. Glenn usually waited until I came on duty, then he would bring us juice and some of Irene's fabulous Danish pastry, and we would eat together at the desk. "It's almost as though none of it ever happened," I said to Glenn.

"That's one of the blessings of being young," he answered. "You can fall in love over and over and, although you think at the time you'll never survive the heartbreak, pretty soon you're ready to try a new romance.''

"It sounds to me as if you've been through a few heartbreaks yourself,'' I said, wishing I could read his mind. Although he had tiny lines around his eyes, his face looked as smooth as Bret's. He really is quite nice-looking, I thought—for a blond. "You must be very old,'' I teased, "to have had so much experience.''

He looked at me with half-closed eyes. "Old enough,'' he said. He sat up straighter. "I'd better get busy. I've rented a chain saw to cut down some of those big limbs.'' I watched him stand up and stretch. The coveralls didn't completely hide his superb build. "I hope you're really over Dennis, Misty.'' He flicked a glance toward their living quarters where Dennis was still asleep, then he frowned slightly at me. "I hated to see you become involved with a . . .'' He looked down at his shoes, then leaned over and re-tied one of them.

"With a what?'' I prompted.

He drew in a deep breath and for a moment I thought he was going to leave without finishing the sentence. "A compulsive gambler,'' he finally said. "He's been like this for years. Aunt Frances tried to get him to quit. So did my dad and mother.'' Then he grinned crookedly. "And believe it or not, Irene's even tried to get him to go to Gamblers' Anonymous!'' He shook his head. "Such a lot of talent going down the drain.'' He sat down again, leaned back, and crossed his legs. "I really thought this place would straighten him out. You heard Irene say that he got fired from the club?''

I nodded.

"I told him he could run this place. I really need him. But I told him no gambling. Now he's started again, and I don't know what to do.'' Glenn sighed deeply and rubbed his hands together. "I've even told him that he needed to be saved, but he told me to go preach to somebody else." He stood up and looked down at me. "Speaking of preaching—I'll be giving the message next Sunday. Want to come?"

A compulsive gambler! I was still stunned at the thought of Dennis's problem. It was hard to believe, and yet I remembered how brightly his eyes had burned that night in the private club, and how angry he was when I didn't want to stay in the gambling room. It must be terrible to feel compelled to gamble. I couldn't imagine it. I could understand a physical addiction to something you put in your body, but the desire to gamble was a mental addiction.

"Yoo hoo, Misty!" Glenn teased.

I looked up at him. "Oh! Of course I want to hear you preach!"

The Community Church was only a few blocks away, and we could have walked, but we rode over in Glenn's silver Honda. We drove into the parking lot almost before I had the seat belt fastened. The church building was cream-colored stucco, with a white steeple and white front doors. There were pines and cottonwood trees on the property, and a few rose bushes that looked as though they hadn't been pruned for years. The yard looked neglected, too, and I thought of Mary Jo's place. In fact, the whole community seemed to be neglected. What a shame, I thought. Donnerville was a beautiful mountain town, and it was dying.

"Do you know Mary Jo?" I asked as we walked toward the foyer.

"Mary Jo Bennett? Sure. Nice lady. Why?"

"You knew that Dennis and I had breakfast there? Well, Dennis told her he wanted to talk over some business with her."

Glenn frowned and pursed his lips. "Can't imagine what business Dennis would have with Mary Jo. Well, no matter. I've got to get my mind on the sermon."

Inside, several people were standing around and talking. As though at a silent signal they stopped and stared at me. Although I had dressed carefully in my blue, ruffled dress, I felt self-conscious. I glanced at my shoulders to see if my slip straps were showing. Had I worn too much eye shadow? Did my hair look all right? I smiled, but my lip quivered. One old lady, dressed all in black, including a funny-looking hat, stepped forward, smiling and eyes sparkling. "Good morning, dear! Welcome! Hello, Glenn! Can't wait to hear you preach." She turned to me conspiratorially and whispered, "Glenn was in my third-grade Sunday school class."

He introduced her, along with several others. Then he escorted me down the aisle to the first row. "I want you here, so I can keep an eye on you," he whispered. His lips touched my cheek, and he squeezed my shoulder.

"I'll be good," I promised, smiling. Glenn was wearing an Oxford gray pin-stripe suit, a white shirt, and a dark red tie. "By the way—you really look nice this morning."

He flashed a smile. "So do you." He bounded up on the platform just as a small choir filed in. One of the elders or deacons (I can never remember which is which), asked the congregation to stand, and we all sang, "Praise God From Whom All Blessings Flow."

During the announcements I looked around at the sanctuary. It was small, but beautiful, with arched, stained-glass windows. I especially admired the one over the baptistry, which showed Christ at the helm of a ship. I glanced toward the back and—why I thought such a thing, I don't know—I could see myself, all in white, walking down the center aisle toward that window. During the special music, a very good solo by a teen-age girl, I looked up at Glenn and found him looking at me. He had a pleasant, slightly dreamy expression on his face. I smiled at him, but he looked away.

His sermon was interesting and thought-provoking. In fact, I completely forgot that Glenn was speaking, and concentrated on the message. He spoke with authority and backed up what he said with passages of Scripture. One thing he said both impressed and troubled me. "If you're a Christian," he said, "you've been created to fulfill a certain function in the body of Christ." He seemed to be looking directly at me. "And if you're not doing it, you're fouling up the plan."

After church, most of the fifty or sixty people came over to meet me. They all seemed glad I had come. Glenn was busy shaking hands at the door. Once, when I looked over at him, he actually seemed to be glowing. I had never seen him look so happy, or so much at peace. *This must be his function in the body of Christ,* I thought. *But what is mine?*

In the car, Glenn said, "Instead of eating at the inn today, how would you like to go up to Mary Jo's? I've never eaten there—I mean, not since she's opened her home to the public."

"I'd love it—but I'm sure it costs a lot, and I can't afford it."

He touched my hand. "I'm buying! It's the least I can do for all your extra work."

"I'm not complaining." I raised an eyebrow and grinned at him. "Not that I want to make a career of working for room and board."

"Come on, now. Don't rub it in." He started the engine. "Anyway, I think you're going to be on the payroll starting next Monday."

"Really? How do you know?"

"A couple of things. We got reservations yesterday for a marriage encounter seminar that will be held the first week in August, and they included a substantial deposit."

"Oh, how wonderful!"

"And a small writers' club in San Francisco has made reservations for a three-day conference, starting August fifteenth."

"How did these people know about our inn? Is it from some of Dennis's contacts?"

"The writers' conference was from his efforts—but the marriage encounter thing came through one of my seminary buddies."

As we turned into Mary Jo's driveway, Glenn said, "Want to hear my favorite dream?"

I turned to look at him. "Of course. What?"

"My favorite dream is to turn the hotel into a Christian conference center." He glanced at me expectantly.

I bit my lip while I groped for a proper response. What did I know about Christian conference areas? I had gone to camp a few times when I was young. I remembered the dormitories, and being homesick, and making macramé. But I had never been in a place that looked anything like the Royce Inn. "How would you go about doing something like that?" I finally asked. "I mean, what would happen to Dennis?" I snickered. "He'd rather die than work with a bunch of religious people!"

"I'm sure you're right," Glenn said.

"You'd have to get a whole new crew—I don't think Candy would stay, or Irene!" I shook my head. "Whew!"

"How about you, Misty? Would you stay?" His green eyes looked into mine so intently I had to look away.

"Well, Glenn," I hedged. I tried to imagine what it would be like to work in a Christian resort. Would I be teaching little kids how to make macramé? Helping little old ladies in black hats and tennis shoes? I answered softly. "You know that, even if I stay this summer, I hope someday to go back to Sorensen."

"But you don't plan to make that a lifelong career, do you?" His heart was in his eyes and, at that moment, I realized Glenn was in love with me! How awful. I felt sorry for him. He was a wonderful, kind, intelligent, yes, even good-looking man, and he had been a loyal friend. But he just wasn't for me. We didn't have anything in common. He was completely wrapped up in church affairs, while I . . . Did I want a career in the business world? Not for the rest of my life. Did I, like Debbie, want to be famous and run around with the "beautiful people?" Heavens, no. What then? Did I—be honest, Misty—did I still want to be Dave's wife? Glenn's pleading look jogged me into answering. "I couldn't possibly know what I'll be doing next summer, Glenn," I said. I looked steadily at the front porch so I wouldn't have to see the disappointment in his eyes.

We walked into Mary Jo's house. On the way Glenn motioned toward three other cars. "She must be getting some Sunday trade, anyway," he said.

"Does it worry you?"

"I suppose it should. But after all, Mary Jo is a widow. I can't begrudge her a living, even if it cuts into our business."

Mary Jo was delighted to see us and kissed us both.

"Where are your boots?" Glenn asked, grinning.

She lifted her chin and laughed. "I think I ought to dress up once in a while—at least on Sunday!" Her white hair was arranged in bouffant curls on top of her head, and she was wearing a black, princess-style dress, and high-heeled black pumps.

"You look wonderful," I said.

"Smell good, too," Glenn added.

She rolled her eyes. "He's the biggest tease in the world, Misty."

There were several people at the big table, and they were apparently celebrating someone's anniversary. Glenn greeted them, but didn't introduce me. We sat at the same table where Dennis and I had had breakfast that morning. The birds were still eating outside the window. "It must cost a fortune to feed those birds," I remarked.

"Yes, it does," Mary Jo admitted, "but doesn't everything that brings pleasure cost something?" The sadness crept into her eyes for a second. Then she smiled and told us what she had prepared for Sunday's menu.

After a satisfying meal of pot roast and vegetables, chocolate cake and ice cream, Glenn motioned to Mary Jo. She came to our table, smiling. "More coffee?"

"No, Mary Jo. I was just wondering if Dennis spoke to you about that—business."

Her eyes widened, and I'm sure mine did, too. I didn't know Glenn could be so devious.

"Why, yes, he did." Mary Jo said. "I didn't realize he had told you."

Glenn looked down at the tablecloth and picked up a spoon. "What was your—opinion?" he asked.

"My opinion?" Her serene features suddenly changed to disgust. "I'll tell you, Glenn, just as I told your cousin. I'm not interested!"

"Good for you!" Glenn chuckled. "Now tell me, Mary Jo, what was his proposition?"

Her mouth dropped open, then her eyes twinkled. "You scoundrel! I should have known you wouldn't have any part of it." She looked around at her other guests, then leaned closer to the table, and whispered, "Dennis wanted to use this house for a casino!"

Glenn's expression was noncommittal, but I was sure the news hurt him. I knew he loved his cousin.

On the way to the car, I asked, "Are you going to tell Dennis that you know his plan?"

"No. I don't want to hurt Mary Jo. Dennis can be ugly. But I've got to figure a way to reach him before he ruins himself—and me." He started the engine, then looked at me. "I'm not ready to go back to work. How about you? Would you like to take a drive?"

I shrugged. "Whatever you want, Glenn. You know when you have to be back."

"I think old Dennis owes me an hour or two. How would you like to drive over to Donner Memorial Park?"

"Fine. Dennis said it was something I should see. Is it far?"

"No. It'll only take about thirty minutes."

"I remember something about the Donner party. Didn't a lot of people die from the cold or hunger?"

"I've forgotten some of the details, too, but I think there were nearly a hundred people originally," Glenn said. "They came from Iowa and Illinois, and probably other states, all trying to get over these Sierra Nevada mountains to California."

Instead of driving back toward Donnerville, Glenn continued on the narrow road past Mary Jo's house, climbing a steep grade. In a few minutes we were on a wider pavement, heading south. "Evidently they thought California was always sunny, with plentiful food, because they weren't prepared for the deep snows and killing temperatures—and 1846 turned out to be the worst winter in thirty years."

"I wouldn't have made a very good pioneer," I shivered. "I hate to be cold." He glanced at me, and I immediately regretted the comment and moved further away on my side of the car.

We had been climbing from the time we left Mary Jo's and were about to reach the summit. "How high are we?" I asked.

"About nine thousand feet," Glenn answered. He stopped the car at a wide place in the road and pointed. "See right through that gap in the hills? That's the original Donner Pass." We sat in silence for a moment while I studied the majestic scene below. "The new highway is over to the right."

"Did all of the people die?" I asked.

"No," he answered. "At first they were divided up in three groups, and some of them got discouraged by the weather and the terrible ordeal ahead, so they stayed where they were. They were all living in three cabins. Some of them—I don't know how many—started out with their wagons and then had to abandon them, because the snow was five- and six-feet deep."

"You mean they were trying to walk in the snow?"

He nodded. "Women and children, too."

He glanced over at me. "The snow around here gets unbelievably deep. Great skiing area."

I looked again at the grass-covered hills, which were spring-green. "It's hard to imagine this place buried in snow."

Glenn went on with his story. "The travelers stayed in the cabins, hoping the weather would moderate and melt the snow. But everything got worse. Somebody let their few animals loose, and the poor beasts wandered off in search of food and died. When the Donner party realized that something was going to have to be done or they'd all starve that winter, seventeen people, including five women, started out to try to cross the pass. Two of the fellows went back that same day, but the others went on."

"The women didn't turn back?"

Glenn looked at me and nodded. "Pretty remarkable, I agree. I don't remember how long they were on the road, but eventually four of the men died—and the others resorted to cannibalism."

"Oh, no!"

"And evidence was later found, back at the cabins, that there was cannibalism there, too."

I shuddered.

"When it was finally over, I think only two of the men survived—but the five women lived." He began to slow down and I realized we were almost there. "Only about half of the party survived," Glenn said as he parked the Honda.

He got out and came around to help me. It was cold, and although I didn't want to do anything to encourage him, I welcomed his arm around my waist as we walked over to look at the Pioneer Monument. It was a rock structure about thirty feet high, with bronze statues of a man, woman and two children on top. The man was shading his eyes as he pressed on, and his wife was beside him, also in a forward stance. Together we read the bronze plaque: "Virile to risk and find—Kindly withal and a ready help—Facing the brunt of fate—Indomitable—Unafraid." Solemnly we walked around the memorial and read the inscription on the back: "In commemoration of the pioneers who crossed the plains to settle California . . . Dedicated June 6, 1918."

"Those people suffered so much," I said quietly.

Glenn squeezed me. "God gives us the power to endure trials when they come." In the car he looked at me gravely. "I believe you would have made a fine pioneer woman."

We took highway 80 back to the Inn, past Donner Lake, through Truckee. In a little while we turned into the driveway of the inn. We didn't go in the back door. Glenn reached for me and we walked hand-in-hand up the driveway to the front.

When we walked into the lobby, Dennis was waiting for us. His dark eyes were narrowed, and he looked angry. "Glenn, the cash doesn't balance." He glanced at me, then back at Glenn. "I've gone over Friday's and Saturday's registrations twice, and both times it comes out fifty dollars short."

CHAPTER 14

AT FIRST DENNIS'S STATEMENT didn't upset me, for I was sure there was an explanation. But when I realized he was really agitated and ready to blame someone, I bristled, too. He was certainly acting high and mighty for a man who had tried to get a widow to turn her home into an illegal gambling operation. He had probably made the mistake himself. Glenn echoed my thoughts.

"Are you sure you haven't added wrong?" he asked, taking the journal from Dennis who gave Glenn a scathing look. "No offense," Glenn soothed. "I just thought possibly you had entered a registration twice, or perhaps counted some travelers' checks as tens instead of twenties. I'm sure there's a simple explanation." He grinned and tapped his cousin's arm lightly with a fist. "Sure you haven't absconded with the funds?"

"Hah!" Dennis grunted. "If I ever abscond with the funds, it won't be for nickels and dimes."

"Well—I don't know where it is. And, actually, fifty dollars is no big deal."

"True, it's no big deal," Dennis answered. "But where is it? Have we a thief in the house?" He didn't look directly at me, but I caught the implication. How dare he accuse me? I drew myself up as tall as I could and said, "It's entirely possible that I've made a mistake in making change. But I'm not the only one who works at the desk and, if my service isn't satisfactory . . ."

"Oh, hush, Misty," Glenn murmured. "No one's accusing you. So we've lost fifty dollars. I say forget it."

"Forget it!" Dennis roared. "That's like turning off the vacancy sign!"

Glenn looked straight into Dennis's eyes. "The matter is closed."

He started back toward his room, then called over his shoulder. "I'll take over, Dennis, just as soon as I change clothes."

Left alone with Dennis I was self-conscious, and acutely aware of his nearness and masculinity. I looked up into his dark, angry eyes.

"Dennis, I have no idea how this happened. But if you feel it's my fault, you can take it out of my first week's pay. Glenn told me I'd be on salary starting next Monday."

His eyes softened. "I don't know how it happened, Misty, and I doubt if it's your fault. I told Irene just last night that you were probably the most valuable employee we had." He patted my arm. "Let's just all be more careful, okay? Fifty dollars isn't a lot, but at this point we can't be throwing away a dime."

I nodded, but couldn't help wondering how much he had thrown away gambling. As I started up the stairs he called after me softly, "You look lovely today." My heart took a tiny dive, and I looked back at him, smiling radiantly.

In my room I unbuttoned my dress and stepped out of it. It was made of black voile with tiny white dots, and a lacy, white collar. I hugged it to me. "Mother was right," I whispered to the mirror. "She said nothing looks as dressy as black and white." Dennis had said I looked lovely!

I felt warm and happy as I put on a one-piece, blue bathing suit. It was more modest than some. At least, it covered top and bottom. I put on a white terry cover-up, picked up a magazine on interior decorating, and went downstairs. I didn't have to work on Sundays, and Glenn had urged me to get out of doors whenever I could. I didn't need to be pushed, because I loved the sun.

I stopped by the desk and told Glenn the same thing I'd told Dennis—that I'd be willing to pay the fifty dollars out of my first paycheck.

"No way, Misty. It was a mistake. From now on, don't mention it, okay?" He put his hand on my arm and squeezed gently. I moved away and thanked him. Poor fellow. I must not give him any encouragement.

Although the pool wasn't filled yet, I went to that area, because the deck was now clean and it was the best place to take a sunbath.

As I lay in the sun on one of the old, but comfortable chaise lounges, I thought about Dave, Dennis, and Glenn. Dave had hurt me a great deal, yet sometimes I thought I still loved him. Dennis had also hurt me, but the moment he said something sweet, I was all aglow again—even though I knew he was a gambler! What kind of a person was I? And here was poor Glenn, obviously in love with me, but all I felt for him was friendship. I enjoyed his sense of humor, and was impressed with his preaching, and although he wasn't my type, he was good-looking. But he didn't excite me. *Too bad,* I thought sleepily. *He'll make somebody a good husband.* I turned over and let the hot rays of the sun warm my back.

"Misty?" I felt a touch on my arm. I opened my eyes and,

117

for a moment, I couldn't remember where I was. I was cold, and it was almost dark. "Misty, you'll get sick again if you don't come in." I turned over and found Dennis smiling down at me. I sat up, and he took my hand. Then he pulled me up. For a moment I thought he was going to take me in his arms, but he let go of me, then placed the beach jacket around my shoulders. "Glenn asked me to come get you."

We strolled toward the front door and, when we started up the steps, he took my arm. We walked in the lobby. Irene was sitting behind the desk, talking to Glenn. When she saw us she stopped in mid-sentence. Her hard eyes took in my bathing suit, and Dennis holding my arm. Flustered, I ducked my head, hurried past the desk, and raced upstairs.

Instead of going to my room, I went to Candy's door and knocked.

"Nobody here," she said.

I opened the door and went in. She was in shorts and halter, lying on the bed, reading. Her room, although larger than mine, was a total disaster. Her clothes were everywhere, books and magazines stacked on chairs, soft drink bottles and beer cans on the dresser and chest of drawers. The closet door was open, displaying a large wardrobe. "What are you doing?" I asked.

"Playing cards with the King of Siam," she answered sarcastically.

"Want to go roller skating?"

"Sure!" She sat up and yawned. "I was just about to be bored to sleep."

"I'll put on jeans and meet you in a couple of minutes."

The roller rink was actually the Elks Club and, on the nights the Elks had dances, there wasn't any roller skating. I had gone skating a couple of times since I'd lived in Donnerville, and both times there were never more than about fifty people skating around. Most of the trade was from high school and younger kids. There hadn't been any eligible men around, but that didn't bother us much. We both enjoyed skating, and we were pretty good, too. I could dance fairly well, and Candy was absolutely marvelous at skating backwards. Bret and Rick were there, clomping around, yelling, and falling down a lot. A fellow about thirty or thirty-five, with a bushy mustache and sideburns and wearing an oil-spotted Stetson, asked me to skate during "Couples."

"Go ahead," Candy whispered. "It's the best offer we've had."

JayDee was a good skater, and it was exhilarating to whirl in and out, our hands clasped, bending and swaying to the rhythm of the music.

When the set was over, he insisted on buying Candy and me a soft drink. We learned he had been born and raised in the area, was divorced, and owned a small ranch outside of town. He knew both Glenn and Dennis, "—although they was jist tadpoles when I was in high school." He pushed his cowboy hat back on his head and stuck his tongue in his cheek while he remembered. "The Royces was always good people," he said. "'Course Dennis was a little wild, and got into quite a scrape in Reno awhile back."

"Really?" I tried to sound casual. "How?"

"Can't remember all of it. He was workin' for some gambling house, and if I'm not mistaken, I believe he was accused of embezzlement."

"I knew anybody as good-lookin' as that dude had to have something wrong with him," Candy said.

"Well, what happened?" I asked. "Did he have to go to jail, or what?"

"No, no. I don't quite remember all the details, but I don't think the house pressed charges—I don't know how he got out of it."

When the rink closed, we had a little bit of a problem making JayDee understand that we didn't want to go someplace else for a few drinks. But we finally got rid of him and, on the way home, I told Candy about the missing fifty dollars. "And do you know, Dennis practically accused me of taking it?" I finished.

"He must have taken it himself," Candy said with conviction.

"But, Candy, if he did, why would he even mention it? He's at the desk when most of the business comes in. He could take whatever he wanted and never say anything."

She shrugged. "I don't know. Sometimes white folks act strange."

I laughed and poked her in the ribs. "Well, one thing is for sure. From now on I'm going to count the money when I come on duty, and have Mr. Parker count it when I go off."

"Right. And I'll keep my eyeballs peeled, too."

The next couple of weeks went by swiftly. Every day the number of tourists increased. Glenn had to hire another maid to help make up the rooms, and I was so busy all the time that, when Dennis came on duty, I was too tired to go anywhere. I usually made myself a sandwich to take to my room, where I'd eat, shower, watch a little TV, and fall asleep. A couple of evenings I had called Mother, and a few times Glenn invited me to go to evening church, but I had declined. I was determined to stay away from him. He was too nice to get hurt, and it was obvious that he cared for me. I wasn't going to do or say anything to lead him on as Dennis had me.

One evening when Dennis came on duty, he said, "Misty, I wish you'd stop this ritual of making me count the money. I trust you."

"I know. But I sleep better at night, knowing that my receipts tally."

He counted the money. He paused, then counted the names in the hotel register, and then the money again. He bit his lip.

"What's wrong?" I asked, with mounting anxiety. Out of the corner of my eye I saw Glenn come in from outside and stop at the counter.

Dennis took a deep breath and looked up at me, then at Glenn. "Short," he said quietly. "Sixty-five."

My pulse was beating in my throat. "It can't be! I'm always super-careful!"

Glenn came around the desk, took the money, and counted it. Then he examined the register. He pursed his lips. "Sixty-five dollars short," he said. "Misty, did you leave the desk today?"

"Of course, but Candy took over, and I was back in a couple of minutes."

"Any other times?"

I thought a moment. "I left once today, at about four o'clock. A little German couple couldn't find their room." I looked at Dennis, then at Glenn. "But I couldn't have been gone over a minute or two, because I showed them their room from the head of the stairs." Both men looked skeptical. "Listen!" I said earnestly. "I didn't take the money. I don't know who did, but it wasn't me!" I gave Dennis a cold look, grabbed up my purse, and started to leave. Three twenties and a five-dollar bill fluttered to the floor.

I could feel all the blood drain from my face. For an instant, I thought I would faint. I stared at the money on the floor. How could it have happened?

Dennis leaned over and picked up the bills. Glenn stared at me, a baffled look in his eyes. I couldn't speak. All I could do was shake my head. I went upstairs to my room and fell across the bed.

After a few minutes Glenn knocked and called to me.

When I let him in, he said, "Misty. Why? I would have given you the money. I'd try to give you anything you wanted."

I slumped in a chair and stared at him wildly. "Glenn! I didn't do it! Somebody's—framed me!"

He looked down and frowned. "Misty, I—I care for you—deeply. Please feel free to tell me anything." He stroked my forehead and smoothed my hair. "Are you in trouble? Please don't lie to me. Are you—pregnant?"

I sat up and faced him, my eyes wide. "Pregnant!"

"Well—you were running away when you came here."

"Glenn! You—of all people! You know I'm not like that! I can't believe you would think such a thing! Why won't anybody believe me?"

We stared at each other in shocked silence a few moments, then he got up, shook his head, and slowly left the room.

As in a nightmare, I began to pack my clothes. I couldn't stay here another second.

CHAPTER 15

As I CAME DOWNSTAIRS tugging at my heavy suitcases, I
didn't look toward the desk. I couldn't bear to see the con-
tempt and accusation in Dennis's eyes. Keeping my eyes on
the front door, the only way of escape from the insane
circumstances that had changed my friends into enemies, I
strode forward purposefully. When I saw the tall, dark man
come swinging through the door, I thought it was Dennis. I
glanced back, but he was lounging on the counter, still
eyeing me suspiciously. I gasped when I recognized the
man coming toward me. It was Dave!

We stared at each other. Suddenly my arms felt weak,
and I dropped the suitcases as he rushed toward me.
"Misty!" he whispered, and took me in his arms. I closed
my eyes and collapsed against him, relief and joy coursing
through my body. How wonderful to see him, to feel his
arms around me. He would protect me from my enemies.
Wait a minute! That wasn't true. Dave had betrayed me,
too. I pushed him away. I had no friends. Irene hated me.
Dennis despised me and, for all I knew, Candy might have

123

had something to do with the crazy plot to get me in trouble. Worst of all, Glenn—the one person I thought really cared—didn't believe me.

Dave pulled me back in his arms. "Where are you headed, sugar?" he asked in a low voice. I gazed at him. It had only been six weeks since I'd seen him, but he looked thinner and older, like a stranger.

"How did you find me?" I countered.

"I called your mom."

"That's where I'm going." My voice was cold. "I'm leaving as soon as I can pack my things in the car." As I made this statement, I received a new surge of confidence. I stepped away from him and lifted my chin. "I have to put these suitcases in the trunk, and there are a few more boxes in my room. Excuse me, Dave." I picked up my bags, but he whipped them out of my hands.

"I'll carry them," he said. "Where's the Camaro?"

"Misty!" Dennis commanded. "May I see you a moment?"

I walked slowly over to the desk while Dave stood by, holding the luggage. He wore a snobbish expression I had always disliked.

"Who is that man?" Dennis whispered.

"An old friend." I turned to go.

"Misty—what do you plan to do?"

"I'm going to Stockton, where I should have gone in the first place." My lips felt as though they were drawn up with a string.

"Is that what you want to do?"

"It's what I *have* to do." I hoped the loathing I felt for him showed in my face. "At least my parents believe me."

He studied the counter a moment, then looked at me, and his dark eyes were as disturbing as ever. "It will probably be best for all of us," he said formally. "I want you to know, however, that I don't blame you. Working with cash is a temptation to anyone.''

My eyes widened and I started to protest, but it probably wouldn't have changed his mind. I whirled around, dug in my purse for the car keys, then walked across the lobby. ''I'll bring the car around, Dave.'' I hurried past him toward the door. ''Would you be kind enough to keep an eye on my luggage?'' I glared at Dennis. ''It seems we have a thief in the hotel.'' I flounced out the front door and caught my breath when I saw Dave's old, brown van parked in front. How many good times we'd had in that old wreck.

''Wait a minute,'' he called. He had put down the suitcases, and walked beside me down the steps, and along the driveway toward the parking area. He put his arm around me. ''It's so good to see you, sugar!''

''Really?'' I walked faster to evade his arm. ''And how's Sharon?''

''That's over.'' He tried to take my hand. ''Please, Misty, believe me. It's been rotten without you.'' I glanced over at him. He looked worried, like a little boy who might not get a bike for Christmas. ''Do you have to go to Stockton? Can't you come back to Reno with me?''

I filled my lungs with the clean mountain air. What timing. I was no longer wanted at the Royce Inn, but Dave wanted me back. All I had to do was overlook a few paltry indiscretions, crawl back into his arms, and be safe and secure again.

I couldn't trust myself to speak. I knew from the past that, when I'm hurt and angry, I say horrible things that can never be unsaid, so I kept quiet. But my thoughts were hateful. Did he actually think I would go back with him? I unlocked the Camaro and got under the wheel, leaned over, and unlocked the other door. Dave folded his body to fit, then reached over for me, but I put out my arm. "Nothing has changed, Dave."

"Yes it has, Misty." In the dim light of the parking lot, his eyes were the color of a gas flame, and burning with desire. "I know now I can't be happy without you, Misty. Come back. Oh, baby, please!" He rested his head against mine for an instant, then he turned my chin, and put his lips on mine. It was a long kiss, and I could feel his excitement as his arms tightened, and his breathing accelerated. But I felt nothing. I seemed to be emotionally paralyzed. For weeks I had dreamed of this moment, only to feel absolutely numb when it came.

I started the engine and put the car in reverse. "Dave, I'm not capable of making a decision tonight." I backed carefully, turned and drove out the driveway, probably for the last time.

"Why?" Dave asked. "What's wrong? I know there's something wrong."

In a monotone, I said, "Sixty-five dollars was missing from the cash receipts, and it was found in *my* purse."

He removed his arm from my shoulder. "And they think you took it? I ought to go in there and—"

I gave him a stern look. "Forget it, Dave." I parked the Camaro nose-to-nose with the van. "I don't want any more trouble." I glanced up at the steps, the veranda, the welcoming lobby. I thought of Candy, the good times we'd had roller skating; meals at Mary Jo's; long talks with Glenn; even Irene had one or two good qualities. And Dennis—he would always have a special place in my heart. He was a gentleman, even if he was a scoundrel. Happy memories. But it was over. Somebody in there wanted me out of the way. I looked back at Dave. "I just want to leave here and never come back."

"All right! Come with me! Let me make it up to you."

"What do you mean?"

"Are you going to make me say it? Okay. I'm sorry for the Sharon thing. Can't we pick up where we left off?"

I examined his face, trying to read his thoughts. At last I asked, "Is this a marriage proposal, Dave?"

His eyes widened. One corner of his mouth turned up, and he lifted his long body enough to reach in the back pocket of his tight jeans. He brought out his wallet, and with tongue touching his upper lip, and a wise look, he drew out a tiny square of tissue paper. I watched, hypnotized, as he unfolded it. He held up the promise ring. Even in the dim light from the street, I could see the tiny diamond sparkle. Reaching for my left hand, he slipped it on the third finger. He looked smug and happy. "Now what do you think?" He pulled me as close as he could, with the console in the way, and this time when his soft lips met mine, I tried to feel something.

It was late when we pulled into Reno. It had taken quite a while to carry down all my stuff; not so long to tell Candy and Dennis strained goodbyes. I knew Irene was in the bar, probably aware of what was going on. But she didn't appear, and I didn't feel like going out of my way to see her. I was disappointed, yet thankful, that Glenn had been called to the hospital to visit one of the church members, so I didn't have to face him again. Knowing that he thought I might be pregnant, as well as dishonest, hurt me almost as much as the night I found out about Sharon.

I followed the van's tail lights all the way to Reno, and my mind whirled. I was going back to Reno to live. I was wearing the promise ring. Dave really loved me and was ready to get married. My dream was going to end happily after all, but why wasn't I happy? *Oh, Misty!* I scolded myself. *Why are you always analyzing your feelings?*

You've been hurt, sure, but you're not the first to be falsely accused. Forget it, and go for the future!

Gradually a general feeling of light-heartedness took over and, as we crossed the Nevada state line, I discovered I was smiling. The glow of Reno's lights added to my euphoria. Think of it! Dave loved me!

My excitement mounted as we drove through the familiar streets, although I was ruefully reminded of the night Dennis and I had a date. What a fiasco! And what a nincompoop I'd been. I was startled out of my reverie when I realized Dave was turning into the parking lot in back of his apartment house. Why was he stopping here? We hadn't discussed it, but I had assumed he would take me directly to a motel, then go home. I pulled in behind him, but kept the engine running. I watched as he got out of his van and locked it. He came over to my window. "You can park right down there, sugar." He pointed to a space about three cars away.

Frowning, I asked, "Aren't you going to help me find a motel?" He looked baffled, and I felt sudden tears springing to my eyes. He was going to let me find my own room. I swallowed hard. "I guess you're tired—that's okay. There's no need for you to drive over there, too."

His mouth opened. "What are you talking about?" You're staying with me tonight."

My throat ached. I searched his eyes to see if he were teasing, but they were wide and serious. He actually expected me to get out of the car and go to his apartment. He had tricked me again.

"Dave," my voice sounded like a little girl's. "You said—you said you were ready to get married."

He put his head in the window and kissed my lips. "Babe, be reasonable. You know we can't be married tonight—oh, I suppose we could, but that isn't the way you want it, is it?"

I turned away. Through the windshield I could see a neat row of aluminum trash barrels and wondered how many broken dreams had been tossed in them. When was I going to learn that, in life, dreams don't come true? Life was hard, made up of facts. And the fact was that I had lost Dave once because of my prudishness. Was I going to throw away this second chance?

I parked, reached in the back seat for my overnight case, locked the Camaro, then walked beside him through a narrow passage and up a wrought-iron stairway. I stood silently while he unlocked the door.

Twice before I had been in Dave's apartment. The day he moved in, I had helped carry up some boxes. That day I'd been as worried as a child waiting to be vaccinated. I almost smiled as I recalled how quickly I'd put down the boxes, and scooted back downstairs. I was not about to be alone with Dave in his new apartment. The second time, we gave a shower for some friends who were getting married. I stewed all evening, wondering what would happen after everyone went home and Dave and I were left alone. But he drank too much wine that night and got sick. By the time I had done the dishes, he was asleep.

Dave snapped on the lights, and, as I stepped inside, I exclaimed. "I don't remember it looking like this! You've got new drapes—and new furniture! I love rattan!" He smiled with pride and turned on the lamps at each end of the couch. The floor was carpeted in a warm tan, a perfect background for the muted brown-and-beige figured cushions. The dining area was also furnished with a rattan game table and four chairs. "Dave! I'm impressed. You have very good taste."

He turned on the stereo and soft music filled the room. There were some nice paintings on the walls, and an expensive alabaster bust on one of the tables. "How did you buy all these things?" I picked up a small vase that looked like jade. I knew his part-time job didn't pay big money. He put his arms around me, drew me against his body and kissed me, gently at first, then almost harshly. I broke away and raised an eyebrow. "Come on, Dave, did you hit a thousand-dollar jackpot somewhere?"

"Oh, Misty. I don't know why we have to talk finances at a time like this. You know I get an annuity from my grandmother."

"No, I didn't know that."

"Sure, you did. You've just forgotten. I've gotten a monthly check ever since the will was settled, about three years ago." He pulled me close again and kissed the top of my head. "Come see the bedroom." He put his arm around my waist and guided me through the door.

"A waterbed!" I was amazed as I took in the sprawling piece of furniture. Somehow, I had always pictured Dave sleeping on a twin bed. A breathless, trapped feeling constricted my chest, but I waved it away. I had made my choice in the parking lot.

"Try it!" Dave sat down, and the velvet patchwork spread rippled and swelled. I eased down beside him. "Lean back," he murmured, and pushed me gently.

"It feels like an air mattress." My attention was drawn to the ceiling where I saw myself. "Do you think your grandmother knows you spent her money on mirrors for the ceiling?"

He laughed a throaty laugh and put his arms around me.

"Misty, my little Misty—" His lips brushed my hair. "I've dreamed of having you right here, in my arms." He looked deep into my eyes, touched my face with warm fingers, then let his hand rest on my throat. He kissed my eyes, then his lips parted and covered mine. He pressed his body against me, and I could feel the urgency of his love.

This is the way to go, I thought. *Dave loves me, and I love him. This is life. This is real. The Royce Inn was only a bad dream.*

Dave was trying to unbutton my shirt. I heard him say, "Why don't we get comfortable?"

CHAPTER 16

DAVE'S FACE WAS FLUSHED as he slowly pulled away from me. "I'll only be a couple of minutes." He leaned over and kissed my eyelids, then bounded off the bed. I sat up and watched him go into the bathroom and close the door.

I glanced around the bedroom. The dresser and chest-of-drawers of heavy carved oak were as impressive as the bed. Thoughts began to tumble around in my mind like clothes in a dryer. This furniture was expensive. Dave had never mentioned extra income from his grandmother. In fact, the main reason he hadn't wanted to get married was that he couldn't afford it. He had tricked me tonight. True, he hadn't said he'd marry me in those exact words, but he'd let me believe that's what he meant. I looked down at the promise ring and turned it around on my finger. My hands were icy. I stood up and looked at my reflection in the huge, plate glass mirror on the dresser. A hollow-eyed, straggly blonde, face blotched from rough kisses, faced me. In my imagination I heard a voice:

If you're not fulfilling the function for which you were created, then the whole body of Christ suffers . . ."

Glenn's words. I could almost see his earnest face, his green eyes, his smile.

I peered into the mirror at the pale, frightened stranger and uttered a moan. "Oh, God! What am I doing here?"

"What did you say, sugar?"

I saw Dave's reflection in the mirror as he came toward me. He had on only a tiger-striped bikini. I had seen him many times in swim trunks or tennis shorts, and never thought anything about it, but now his nakedness was an affront. I looked down at my hands and twisted the ring off my finger. I placed it on the dresser.

"I'm leaving, Dave." I reached for my overnight case, but he caught me in strong arms, spun me around, and kissed me savagely. He had on a strong musk cologne that sickened me. I fought him, but he was too strong. I choked back a scream as I struggled to get loose.

I had to get away from Dave before it was too late! When I no longer resisted, he let me go. I touched my lips. I could taste blood.

"What do you mean, you're leaving?" His breathing was rapid, and his facial expression ugly.

"Just that. I'm leaving. There's your ring."

"Look!" He grabbed my wrist. "You don't just kiss me off like that."

I was about to stamp on his bare foot with a high heel when I remembered Glenn saying, "You can't fault a man for being a man." My wrist hurt, but I looked up at him calmly. "Dave, let's don't completely ruin our friendship." He continued to glare at me for another second or two, then dropped my arm. "And I want to ask you to forgive me for leading you on tonight." I was amazed at the maturity in my voice.

Dave's eyes were unbelieving as he backed up and sat down on the bed.

"I honestly don't know why I'm so Victorian, Dave, but I am." I picked up the overnight case and hung my purse strap over my shoulder. "Goodbye."

He stood up. "Wait. I'll throw on some pants and walk down with you."

"Please don't. I can find my way. I've caused you enough trouble."

He took my fingertips. "Misty—don't go like this." He glanced down at himself and seemed suddenly embarrassed. "I'm sorry I came on so strong. We could probably get married tomorrow."

I pulled away and shook my head, walking through the living room and out into the crisp, night air. As I ran down the steps, my heels made a loud, ringing noise on the metal stairs, and I was sure people were watching me. I ran through the narrow passage to the parking area and quickly unlocked the Camaro, threw the overnight case into the back seat, and started the engine. It was a long way to Stockton and it was already midnight.

When I saw the sign "A ROYAL REST AT THE ROYCE INN" I had an almost overwhelming urge to stop, but I had been an all-around fool for too long. My heart actually hurt as I forced myself to sit up straighter and, with eyes fixed on the highway, I roared by the hotel. When I could see the hotel in my rear-view mirror, I wondered if Glenn were in bed. With a little gasp of disappointment I remembered they were going to fill the swimming pool either today or tomorrow, and I wouldn't be there. Glenn had promised to teach me to dive.

Tears came to my eyes, and I reached over in my purse to find a tissue. Opening my purse reminded me of the sixty-five dollars. I had been so occupied with the accusation, my defense, and then the turmoil with Dave, that I'd never really tried to figure out who would be so vindictive as to want to get rid of me. The daily cash was kept in a locked drawer in the desk, but it was so much trouble to take out a key and unlock the drawer that we had foolishly left the key in the lock. Dennis had warned us after the first fifty dollars disappeared, but Glenn had shrugged it off. "Who comes back here? You, me, Misty, sometimes Candy or Irene."

Of course, it had to be Irene. She had even told me once she'd be looking for an excuse to have me fired. I was tempted to turn around, go back and have it out with her. If it was obvious to me that it was Irene, then wasn't it obvious to Glenn and Dennis? And yet neither of them had rushed to my defense. On the contrary, they both acted as though they were convinced I had taken the money. However, when I looked at it objectively, I had to admit the evidence was incriminating. Besides, both of them had known Irene long before they knew me. She had evidently been trustworthy in the past. Nevertheless, I was convinced Irene had framed me.

In Sacramento I stopped at a coffee shop. My eyes felt scratchy, and my legs and back ached. *As much as I hate driving at night, why did I allow myself to get in this bind?* I sighed wearily as I went in and sat down at the counter. "Coffee, please," I said to the waitress. She was large and buxom, with a wide face, brown eyes, and a nice smile.

"On your way to Reno?" she asked, working a toothpick in her lips.

"No, Stockton." I tried to smile, but I didn't feel like it. I didn't feel like talking, either.

"Come next week, me and my boyfriend are going to Reno!" she volunteered. "I can't wait!"

She wore a small diamond on her ring finger. "Are you getting married?"

A sad look came into her eyes. "No—not yet. We're

135

trying to get a down payment on a house so we can move out of the cruddy apartment we're in." She brightened. "When we get that, then we'll get married." She polished the counter with a damp cloth. "No, we're just going to Reno to have some fun." She raised her eyebrows and smiled. "Who knows? We might win enough to make that down payment!"

I smiled. "Who knows?" But I thought, *How stupid!* **Doesn't she know she can't win?** Then I thought of Dennis. *How can anyone as intelligent as he be so stupid about gambling?* But I was just as idiotic about other things. Men, for instance. I suddenly felt thankful and relieved. Except for the grace of God, I would be in Dave's apartment right now—as trapped as this poor girl.

"Do you live in Stockton?" she asked.

Her question startled me. Did I? Where did I live? "Not exactly," I answered. "I've been laid off, and I'm going to visit my folks."

She shook her head sympathetically. "Lot of people out of work." Then she smiled. "If you want to complain about being laid off, you're in the right town! The governor's mansion is just a few blocks from here!" We both laughed.

"I can see myself knocking on his door at this hour!" I said. "Pardon me, sir, but would you please pull a few strings so I can get my job back?" We laughed again.

"Yeah, and while you're at it, Guv,' float a loan for me and my boyfriend so we can get married!"

And Governor, I thought, *would you please straighten up things at Royce Inn so I can go back there for the rest of the summer?* I dreaded to go to Stockton. Why? It wasn't the city. Stockton was all right. What, then? It must be the defeat. I had been so sure of myself a few years ago. Now I had failed at my job in Reno. Failed at love. Failed at Royce Inn.

I was still thinking about these things when I arrived in Stockton. It was still dark, but morning traffic was already heavy on I-5. Monstrous semi-trucks, hauling produce in open trailers, thundered by. They were doing at least sixty-five miles an hour. "Stockton, you're getting more like Los Angeles every day," I said aloud.

It was with relief and exhaustion that I turned the corner of the familiar tree-lined street I had known since I was a little girl, and stopped in front of my parents' home. I supposed it was still my home, although I no longer carried a key. I looked at my watch. By the street light, I could see it was only five o'clock. I drummed my fingers on the steering wheel. Too early to wake Mother and Dad. They wouldn't be up for another hour. I leaned back and closed my eyes.

I must have gone to sleep because the next thing I knew, Dad was backing his car out of the driveway. I leaped out and hurried over to see him. He looked surprised and pleased. "What brings you home, Squirt?" I leaned in the window and kissed his cheek. "You don't have time for me to tell you now," I said. "I'll talk to you tonight." He nodded. "Okay, sweetie. See you then."

I waved to him as he straightened the car and sped away to his job in downtown Stockton. He was a certified public accountant, in business with two other men. I walked across the lawn and glanced over at Mrs. Brown's house. If I knew her, she had probably seen me drive up this morning. When I was in high school, I was positive she could see in the dark.

I skipped up the two steps of the recessed front porch. This entry was one reason Mother wanted the house. "I just love all these bricks, and the redwood and all the exotic plants!" she had exclaimed the first time the real estate agent showed us the place. I was little then and, during my

137

school years, I had accepted my home as a matter of course. Now I eyed the property with new appreciation. It was a beautiful house and Mother and Dad kept it in A-1 condition. It was worth two or three times now what they had paid for it. "Wonder if I'll ever have anything like it?" I mused, as I tapped out our secret knock.

Mother opened the door a crack, then pulled it wide. She and I were the same height, but she seemed shorter in her bedroom slippers. We looked a bit alike and, as I got older, I could see the resemblance myself.

"Why, honey!" She reached out and hugged me. She had on a pink quilted housecoat, and her blondish-gray hair was tousled. "Where'd you come from?" She felt soft when I hugged her, and she smelled yummy. She had always been ultra-feminine.

"It's so good to see you, Mother!" I kissed her and squeezed her tight. "I love you so much!"

"And I love you. I'm so relieved to see you." She pulled me through the hall and into the kitchen. "I've been a little worried about you ever since Dave called. I knew you didn't want to see him, but he sounded so broken up, I couldn't help but tell him where you were." We sat down at the little breakfast table, and within minutes she had placed a bowl of cereal before me, along with milk and a piece of toast. "Do you want coffee or milk?"

"Coffee's fine, Mother. In fact I may go to sleep right here at the table, anyway." I yawned. "I've been up all night." I poured milk on the cereal and was just lifting a spoonful to my mouth when she reached over for my hand. "Let's ask the blessing." For such a long time I had associated with people who didn't say grace that I'd gotten out of the habit. Glenn, of course, always prayed silently and had asked a blessing when we had dinner at Mary Jo's. "Sorry, Mother." I ducked my head while she prayed. It brought tears to my eyes to hear her talking to God as though He were a member of the family.

After breakfast Mother suggested I go to bed, but even though I hadn't slept for twenty-four hours, I knew I was too keyed up to sleep. We took our coffee and went out on the patio. "So far the weather's been pretty good," Mother said. "Warm, but not unbearable." She looked up at blue skies and white clouds. "I dread the hot weather."

"That was the nice thing about the place where I was working," I said. "It was right in the mountains—cool and breezy."

"Well, Misty, I wish you'd start at the beginning and tell me what's been going on. I haven't seen you since Christmas, and you don't say much on the phone."

"I know. One reason I never talked long was because of the cost."

"You could always reverse the charges," she answered. "And that's something else I haven't been able to understand. Why were you at that hotel? I know you were laid off in Reno, but why didn't you come home?"

I sipped my coffee. "Mother, I didn't want you to know all about Dave. Somehow I felt I couldn't tell you." She looked hurt. "You never thought he was good enough for me, anyway!" I laughed and she nodded wisely. "I guess I didn't want to give you the chance to say 'I told you so.'"

I looked beyond the patio to the back yard. Mother liked to putter in the garden. In her flower beds there was probably every kind of flower that would grow in the area. No matter what time of year, she managed to have something blooming. "But, Mother, you had him pegged right," I admitted.

I told her about Dave's fling with Sharon, and my running away from Reno, then losing my billfold and having to stay at the inn. "When Glenn asked me to work, at first it was just going to be for a couple of days . . ."

"But how did you wind up working for nothing?" she interrupted. "I can't understand why you'd do that when you have a college degree and all that experience . . ."

"I know it seems crazy, but at the time it was what I wanted to do." It was already beginning to get hot, and I lifted my hair up off my neck for a moment, then let it fall. "Subconsciously, I think I didn't want to get too far away from Reno. I suppose I hoped all along that Dave would, as you say, repent!"

"He certainly sounded repentant on the phone." She got up, walked to the edge of the patio, leaned down, and pulled a couple of weeds. "Of course, I didn't know anything about that other woman."

"He convinced me last night he was sorry." I shut my eyes for a moment and wished I could shut out the memory. "He was so repentant that I went back to Reno with him." Mother's eyes got big and her mouth opened. I looked down at the concrete floor. Should I tell her everything? That I had actually decided to live with Dave? No, I just couldn't bring myself to confess everything. I smiled slightly. "No, Mummy, I didn't! But he wanted me to. And it was all pretty nasty. So I came running home to you."

"Thank the Lord!" she murmured. "What about the people at the inn? Didn't you leave them in sort of a spot?"

I looked up at the redwood beams and ran my fingers through my hair. "Oh, Mother! I guess I'll just have to tell you the whole story."

I told her what a witch I thought Irene was, and how she had been jealous of me because of Dennis. I told her how handsome he was, and that I'd been "slightly attracted" to him. But I didn't tell her he was a gambler, or about our date in Reno. Then I told her about Glenn and church. "You'd like him, Mother. He's really a fine man." I grinned wryly. "Kind of stuffy, but nice." I told her about

140

Debbie, and Candy, and finally, about the thefts. "So, you see, Mother, they think *I* did it."

"You? How *could* they?"

I raised my eyebrows. "I don't know. I've gone over and over it in my mind. I'm positive it was Irene, but Glenn and Dennis must not think so. The evidence points to me. They obviously don't want a thief on the payroll. So, when Dave came in last night, I jumped at the chance to go back with him."

Mother sat staring at me for a few seconds, a look of concern and pity on her face. "My poor, poor little girl." She started to pat my hand, but I jerked it away. For some reason her motherly solicitude angered me. "I'm not poor. Just stupid, stupid, stupid." I jumped up and walked over to the edge of the patio. I could remember my friend Melissa and me playing in the yard—standing on our heads, doing cartwheels and backbends. It seemed like a million years ago. I turned away. "I think I'll take a shower and crawl into bed. Tomorrow I'll go job-hunting."

CHAPTER 17

FOR THE NEXT WEEK job-hunting became a way of life for me. When Daddy came home from work that first evening, he brought me up to date on Stockton's business world.

"There's a lot of unemployment," he said, "but there are also a lot of job opportunities. The thousand miles of waterways will always give Stockton a little edge."

"I'm not too good at piloting a river boat," I joked.

"No, of course not." He disregarded my feeble joke and continued in a serious voice. "Nevertheless, the waterways bring a lot of fishermen, water skiers, and vacationers to the area. So the resulting businesses—marinas, houseboat rentals, camps, tourist supplies—bring dollars and jobs to Stockton."

I tapped my foot restlessly. "But surely with my education, I can get something better than renting houseboats to rich businessmen," I protested.

"Maybe you could get a government job," Mother injected. "Maybe at Tracy—"

"And, of course, agriculture is and always has been

Stockton's most important resource," Daddy went on as though Mother hadn't said anything.

"What I'm really qualified for is office administration in an engineering company."

Daddy nodded. "I know. One of my accounts works for Standard Oil. Maybe he could find you something in SOHIO. Come down to the office in the morning, and I'll try to make some contacts for you." He reached over and patted my hand. "I'll even take you to lunch."

The next morning I showered, shampooed my hair, and blew it dry. While it was setting in hot rollers, I gave myself a good manicure. I took special care with my make-up. It was important to look just right for the job interviews. I wore a navy blue sleeveless dress made of a crisp, linen-like material. It had a white sailor collar and white piping around the armholes. My hair turned out right for a change, and it hung in loose waves around my shoulders.

I kissed Mother goodbye, got in the car, and started for the freeway. As I drove south on I-5, I was amazed at how many condominiums had gone up just in the last couple of years. Everything looked flat and uninteresting as I sped downtown. How I longed to be in the mountains again!

I got off on Fremont, and found the parking lot Daddy had told me about. My plan was to call on as many engineering firms in the area as I could, then meet him at eleven o'clock. I went to several places, but only filled out two applications. Most personnel offices weren't accepting applications, and I was either over-qualified for the openings available, or not experienced enough in a particular field. Daddy had succeeded in making an appointment for me at SOHIO, but it didn't seem too promising. There were "no openings at the present time."

"Go anyway, baby," Daddy counseled. "When they see how pretty you are, they'll *make* an opening!" He took me around to meet his partners, then we went to lunch.

He took me to the "Castaway," a romantic restaurant overlooking the Delta. I loved the lavish furnishings, the excellent service, and the fabulous salad bar.

"Between Mother and you, I'm going to get fat," I complained, as we sat down at a table next to a window. Outside, the channel water lapped gently against the building. "It's almost like being on a ship," I said. Lunch was fun. The only missing ingredient, I thought, was an eligible man.

Later that afternoon I went to see the druggist who had hired me when I was in high school, but all the summer jobs were taken. "August is a poor time to be looking for work, Misty," he said.

But I kept on trying, even when it seemed hopeless. "I can't even get a hostess job!" I told Mother late one afternoon. We were in the living room, and I had taken off my shoes to rub my burning feet. They felt as though they were on fire from wearing high heels all day.

Mother shook her head. "I don't understand it. I've prayed and prayed for you to find a good job." I gave her a baleful look, but didn't comment. My folks were beginning to get on my nerves. I loved them dearly, but I'd been away from home too long to become their little girl again. "Have you prayed, baby?" she persisted.

"I pray! If you mean—have I asked God specifically for a job—no. I think He has more important things to do."

"Well, honey, that may just be the problem. You know, Jesus loves you even more than I do, and it probably hurts Him when you leave Him out of your life."

"Oh, Mother!" I knew there was a sharp edge in my voice, but I wanted this conversation to end. Without warning, I thought of Glenn. I remembered the night he had prayed for me to get well. I picked up my shoes and forced myself to smile. "What gourmet feast are we having tonight?"

That was another thing that was beginning to get on my nerves. Mother's method of showing love was cooking. Her meals were delicious, but not only was I eating too much, I felt like a leech. If I didn't find a job soon, I would be forced to sign up for unemployment insurance.

"I baked a chicken this morning," she answered. "I thought we'd eat out on the patio."

I went to my room and got out of my clothes. I felt hot, sticky, and irritable. I stayed in the shower for a long time. That was the only place I could count on being alone, as Mother didn't approve of closed doors. "If I think of something I want to tell you," she said the second day I was home, "I don't want to have to come knock on your door." She was so sweet and appealing I couldn't be angry with her, but I realized what a haven little old Number Seven had been.

The shower spray felt wonderful—cooling and cleansing. *If only I could be as clean on the inside*, I thought. "You can," a Presence seemed to whisper. I swallowed and fought back tears, but they came anyway. *Dear God, I haven't left you out of my life on purpose. Forgive me, please. And—oh, God, I really do need a job!"*

That night after dinner, Mother dropped a bombshell.

"Misty, since you haven't had any luck finding work, I told the Vacation Bible School director you might be willing to teach for the next two weeks."

"Mother! How could you do that!"

"Well, honey, I can sense you're getting bored, and I just thought you'd enjoy it." She looked at me with her big eyes, wide and appealing. "They really are in a bind. One of the teachers hurt her back and is going to have surgery."

Reluctantly, the next day I drove to church, the same brown stucco church I'd attended from first grade until I left home.

The director was so overjoyed to have me, and all the other teachers and the kids made me feel so welcome that, even though I'd felt resentful at first, by the end of the first day I was looking forward to going back.

"It's really great to sing the old songs," I told Mother that night. "And the kids are so darling. One little girl told me she thought I was a TV star!"

On the second morning of Bible School, a woman came, holding a little girl by the hand and carrying a baby in her arms. She looked familiar.

"Melissa!" I cried, recognizing my old friend from childhood days.

"Misty!"

We embraced, then I looked at the children. "These aren't yours, are they?"

"Denise isn't," she said, and touched the little girl's head. "She's my niece, and I'm taking care of her for a few days. But this one's mine!" She turned the baby so I could see his round cherub face. "This is Markie."

"He's darling. Markie! Then you married Mark, right?"

She nodded, beaming. Melissa was taller than I, with mousy brown hair. She could never make it do anything in high school, and it looked about the same now. But in her own pale way, she was pretty.

The next two weeks flew by. I looked forward each morning to being with my class—eight darling second-graders.

With them, I memorized the songs and Bible verses. But I also enjoyed being with Melissa and little Mark. She hadn't planned on working at the school, but since there was a nursery, and she had to bring Denise anyway, she decided

146

to help out. We spent our breaks together and, although our lifestyles were miles apart, whatever had attracted us to each other when we were small was apparently still operating.

Melissa had only spent a year at Delta College before she and Mark married, and then she'd gone to work at Weinstock's to help put Mark through school.

"It was hard," she said, "but worth it. There's nothing I'd rather be than Mark's wife, and Markie's mother!"

I shook my head. "Not me! I don't want to be tied down—not yet, anyway." But deep in my heart I knew the emotion I was experiencing was jealousy! "You sound like a good date for Mark's brother," Melissa said. "He's really a nice guy, but marriage is not for him—he says!" She pushed her hair out of her eyes. "Would you like to meet him? I could have you both over for dinner."

I shrugged. "Sure. I'm game if he is."

While Mother, Dad, and I were eating dinner that night, the telephone rang. It was Melissa. "Instead of having dinner here tomorrow night, Paul wants to take us out," she said, with excitement in her voice.

"Paul?" I answered. I had completely forgotten about her plan for me to meet Mark's brother.

"He said it was too hot for me to cook!" She giggled. "He never seemed to notice the heat before when I invited him for dinner! I think he's anxious to make a good impression on *you!*"

"Well, for heaven's sake," I answered—pleased, yet suspicious. "What did you tell him, Melissa?"

"I told him you were a lifelong friend, that we'd been out of touch for the last few years, and that you'd been living in Reno. That's all." She paused. "Oh—I also mentioned that you were blonde and beautiful."

I groaned. "Now he'll be disappointed."

"No, he won't. I showed him your picture in the high school annual."

"Oh, no! Not that old thing!"

"Listen, he's impressed. He's going to take us to the Hilton!"

When I told Mother and Dad about my blind date, they both seemed happy.

"The Hilton!" Mother cooed. "He must be rich."

"Melissa didn't say what he does for a living."

"The Hilton's a beautiful hotel," Dad said. "Hasn't been up too long."

"What are you going to wear?" Mother asked.

"I don't know. Probably my blue."

"I think she needs a new dress, don't you, Daddy?" Mother's tone was wheedling. "After all—"

"No, I don't!" I exploded. It bothered me that I was living off my parents. "I have plenty of clothes." But Dad reached for his billfold and took out a couple of twenties. He smiled at me. "Will this be enough?"

I frowned at him. "Dad . . ."

"Oh, fiddlesticks," Mother said, and picked up the money. "Just call it an early birthday present." She began to clear off the table. "Help me, Misty, and we'll jump in the car and go over to the mall tonight."

Mother had much more stamina that I did when it came to shopping. We must have gone in and out of a dozen shops, and after an hour of getting in and out of my jeans and trying on dresses, I complained. "Please, Mother, let's call it a night. I don't have to have a new dress."

"Yes, you do," she said, blue eyes twinkling. "This may be the start of something big."

At last we found a dress that pleased us both. It was made of sheer white crepe, with a V neck and a ruffled cape collar. "You look gorgeous, honey!" Mother said. "And I'll let you wear my pearls!"

"Why are you so excited about this date?" I scolded. "I'm not. Besides, Melissa already told me he doesn't want to get serious."

Mother sniffed. "Your father said that, too."

"He's probably ugly," I went on, "with big buck teeth—like this." I wrinkled my nose and lips to expose my front teeth, and Mother gave me her prim look.

"Besides, he's probably bald," I teased, "and shorter than I am."

CHAPTER 18

THE NEXT EVENING AS I was getting dressed I called out, "Mother! Be sure and keep an eye out for Mortimer Snerd!" Although I enjoyed teasing her, I really hoped Paul would be nice-looking. He wouldn't have to be as handsome as Tom Selleck, but it would be nice if he could be a brunet with dark eyes. *Why a brunet, Misty? Who are you thinking of—Dave or Dennis?* Glenn's bright smile and green eyes popped into my mind, and I whispered to the mirror, "Okay! I'll settle for a handsome blond."

I was waiting in the living room, watching the seven o'clock news with Dad, when a dark blue sedan stopped in front. I stood up for a better look. Melissa and two men got out of the car. One was short, sallow, and balding; the other, tall and good-looking. "I knew it," I whispered, scowling.

"What'd you say?" Dad asked.

"Nothing." As they approached, however, I realized Melissa was walking with the short one! I'd never met her Mark, but the way she'd raved about him at Vacation Bible School, I thought he was another Burt Reynolds. The tall, handsome man walked behind them. He wore a tan sport coat, white pants, and white shoes. He stood straight, and walked toward the house with an easy, confident air.

"Mother!" I rasped in a stage whisper. "They're here!"

She rushed into the living room just as the doorbell pealed.

"Hi," I said, opening the screen door.

Melissa kissed my cheek. "Misty, this is my husband, Mark." He smiled shyly, and nodded. "And *this,*" she paused dramatically, "is Paul."

I looked into deep brown, smoldering eyes. His eyebrows were as dark and thick as his hair, and he looked as though he'd spent a lot of time in the sun. He was so handsome I felt a little giddy as he took my hand.

I introduced the men to my parents, then said, "And I know you both remember Melissa." Paul and I stared at each other while Melissa showed Markie's picture to Mother. Then, almost as though we were alone, we floated out to the car. I hoped Paul hadn't seen Mother's knowing wink. I could tell by the crazy sparkle in her eyes that she was delighted with Paul's appearance.

He helped me into the car, closed the back door for Melissa, then hurried around to the driver's side.

"I wanted to drive the Corvette instead of this old Cad," he said, "but Melissa thought you'd be more comfortable if we were all together."

"Old Cad?" I echoed. "It looks new to me!"

"It's a couple of years old." He started the engine and we floated away from the curbing. "Time to trade it off." He pushed in the cigarette lighter, then opened a case which looked like gold, and offered me a cigarette. I shook my head. He put one between his full lips and lit it. When the smoke billowed out, I coughed. I hated cigarettes, and probably wouldn't have accepted the date if Melissa had told me he smoked. On the other hand, according to Dave and Dennis, I was too prudish. I fought down my disappointment, and determined not to hold this one bad habit against him.

I turned around to look at Mark and Melissa. In spite of the hot weather, they were snuggled up to each other.

"I'm so glad I don't have to cook tonight," Melissa said. Her hair tumbled about her shoulders, and she was wearing a pink dress that looked as though it might have been a bridesmaid's dress. She looked pretty—more like sixteen than twenty-three.

"Where are Markie and Denise?" I asked.

"With my mom," she said. "Denise is a doll, but Mark is something else. Hope he goes to sleep for her."

"He will," Mark said. "I love to sleep, and he's *my* son!"

I laughed. "Where do you work, Mark?"

"I'm an engineer. Department of Agriculture," he said.

"Sounds good," I said.

He shrugged and smiled modestly. "It's a job."

I looked at Paul. "Do you work for the government, too?"

"Transportation," he said, smiling over at me.

Mark began to cough but, when I glanced back, he was staring out at the traffic.

Before I had a chance to ask Paul any more questions, he drove into the Hilton parking lot.

I felt a little thrill as he helped me out of the car and we walked toward the hotel entrance. I caught a glimpse of our reflections in the plate glass door. I thought we looked very nice together.

The interior of the hotel was impressive. The guest rooms were arranged around the walls of the structure with railed corridors, leaving a great vaulted ceiling several stories high. People on each floor could look down at the lobby below.

Paul seemed at ease and guided us directly to the Chez Pierre dining room. "This is beautiful," I said as we sat down. "Melissa, look at the walls. They're padded, and covered with fabric."

"And look at the napkins," Melissa said. "They're folded like tulips."

"I often dine here," Paul said. "When you have a position like mine, it pays to entertain at the best places."

"Well, some of us aren't as well-heeled as others," Mark said. He and Melissa looked into each other's eyes, but their faces were expressionless. Paul lit another cigarette and studied the wine list the waiter handed him.

"Bud," Mark said confidentially, "if you're ordering wine for Melissa and me—forget it. We don't drink, remember?"

"Neither do I," I said quickly.

"Surrounded by peasants!" Paul said good-naturedly. "And right in the heart of wine country!" To the waiter he said, "Your house wine, please."

"Look at that armoire!" Melissa whispered to me, and nodded toward a massive piece of furniture with doors made of plate glass mirrors.

"Yes!" I answered. "And the chandeliers!"

"This is nothing compared to some other places I've been," Paul said. "If you stay in Stockton for a while, Misty, I'll take you to some really fine places."

When the waiter brought the wine, I remembered the night in Reno with Dennis, and suddenly felt anxious. I hoped Paul wouldn't drink the whole bottle.

At Paul's insistence that we order anything we wanted, Melissa, Mark and I ordered sirloin steaks.

"Nothing beats a good steak," Mark said.

"I agree! Especially when you eat as much hamburger as we do!"

Paul read the menu carefully. Finally he looked at the waiter and said, "How is the Carre D'Agneau Persille this evening?"

"Tres bien, monsieur."

Mark looked up at the ceiling.

"Good grief, Paul! Why can't you order steak like the rest of us?" Mark asked. Paul ignored the question and said something else to the waiter in French. With a bow, the waiter left. Then Paul turned his attention to me.

"Melissa tells me you're from Reno?"

"Yes and no," I responded. "Stockton is my home, but I lived in Reno until recently."

"My sister-in-law spoke the truth when she said you were beautiful." His voice was low, and he looked directly into my eyes.

I glanced over at her. "She exaggerates."

Paul took my hand. "What small hands you have." He looked closely at my ring finger. "Don't tell me you've recently been engaged?"

I felt my lips open. Then I shrugged. "Not really."

He lifted the palm of my hand to his lips. "I'm glad." He kissed my fingertips. "I wouldn't want any ghosts around to spoil things for us."

I looked at Melissa and she raised an eyebrow at me, our old signal to be careful. Was she warning me about her own brother-in-law? She was the one who had set up this date. Mark buttered a piece of bread deliberately, staring at us, then took a bite.

"Have you ever been on a houseboat?" Paul asked as he released my fingers.

"No, I never have," I answered, glad he had changed the subject. I wasn't used to having my hand kissed, especially

154

not in front of other people. "Isn't that awful, when I've lived here most of my life?"

"I'll have to take you out on my boat," he said. "There's nothing as romantic as a cruise."

"Is it hard to operate a houseboat? They seem so clumsy."

"No—nothing to it. At least, not for me. Of course, my specialty is speedboats." He sipped some wine. "You do water ski, don't you?"

"I've been up on skis, but I'm not very good."

"Oh, well! With my instruction, you'll be an expert in no time."

"Like you, Paul?" Mark asked, a taunting look on his face.

Paul shrugged. "So I had a little spill last year. It wasn't my fault."

"Oh, good," Melissa said hurriedly. "Here's our food."

My steak was cooked to perfection. The waiter kept our glasses filled with ice water, and our cups with hot coffee. The broccoli was steamed and seasoned exactly right for me; the salad, crisp and delicious. I could find nothing wrong with the meal, but Paul sent his soup back because it wasn't hot. He asked for fresh bread, and the waiter had to bring him a different piece of lamb because it wasn't pink enough. All of these complaints made me uncomfortable, but the meal was expensive and, since Paul was paying for it, he should be satisfied.

After our meal, when the dishes were cleared away, Paul lit a cigarette and asked, "Dessert?" I shook my head. "I couldn't!" Melissa also declined, but Mark looked longingly at the dessert cart filled with éclairs, cakes, tortes, and all kinds of pie.

"Go ahead, brother," Paul said magnanimously. "I can afford it! Help yourself."

155

Mark turned back to the table and looked at Paul. "No, thanks. I don't need anything else."

"I know!" Melissa said. "Let's go to our house for dessert. I'm supposed to take cookies to Bible School tomorrow, and I made a whole bunch. And there's ice cream."

"Sounds very nice, Melissa," Paul said.

Her cookies were good, although I could eat only one. We sat in their small living room and talked awhile—that is, Melissa and I talked. The two brothers were complete opposites. They didn't look alike or talk alike, and they didn't seem to like each other very much.

I glanced at my watch. "Goodness, it's after ten! We have to be at church early tomorrow, remember?" I said to Melissa. "It's the last day."

"Which means rehearsal for the children's program," she added.

Paul stood up. "In that case, Misty, I'd better take you home."

We said our goodnights, then Paul helped me into the car. As he closed the door, I was suddenly afraid. This would be my first time alone with him. The car smelled like stale smoke, and I tried to open a window. Then I remembered that they were electrically operated, so the ignition key would have to be on. When Paul got in on the driver's side and lit a cigarette, I opened my window a crack.

"No need to do that," he said. "The air conditioner will cool it off in a minute."

"I'm not too warm," I said, "It's just that—" I didn't finish the sentence since I didn't want to be a complainer. It would only take about five or ten minutes to get home. I could stand the smoke that long. Instead of turning north on Pacific toward my parents' home, however, Paul turned south. "Haven't you made a mistake?"

"I don't believe so." He looked at me, smiling. He put his arm around my shoulder and pulled me close.

I moved away gently. "I think you have. I live in Lincoln Village, remember?"

"Of course." He pulled me close again. At the University he made a series of turns and I lost my sense of direction. For a moment I was terrified. Women were always getting raped or murdered. But Paul was Melissa's brother-in-law. They were decent people. She would never have suggested this date if there were anything wrong with him, would she? I forced myself to be calm, and tried to get my bearings. Stockton had changed a great deal, but I had never seen this part of town. At last I read a street sign, "Monte Diablo." Even the name gave me the shivers. "Where are we going?" I asked.

"You'll see. We're almost there."

We came to a park, and he headed the Cadillac into an open place which overlooked the channel. He turned off the engine and looked at me intensely.

"I wanted you to see the channel at night. Especially since there's a full moon."

"It's beautiful," I said. "Is that an ocean liner?"

"A cargo ship. They can come all the way from the Pacific Ocean. Isn't that amazing?"

"It surely is." I began to relax. He wouldn't try anything on the first date. But suddenly he put his arms around me in a crushing embrace, and almost smothered me with a long disgusting kiss. Even though I pushed with all my strength, I couldn't break free. His hands began to fumble with my dress, and I regretted that I had chosen a V-neck. "Please—" I begged, when he paused for breath. "Take me home!"

"Are you kidding?" he whispered, as he kissed my neck and shoulders. His hands were everywhere, and I could hear myself grunting and moaning as I tried to hold on to his thumbs. Silently I prayed, *Oh God, help me!* All at once I felt Mother's strand of pearls break. Despair, then anger flooded me. "Oh, no!" I screamed. "Now look what you've done! You—you maniac!"

"What's wrong?" he panted.

I moved to the far side of the seat. "What's wrong! Look!" I held what was left of the necklace in my hand. "Those are my mother's pearls. My dad gave them to her on their twenty-fifth anniversary! She wanted me to wear them for you!" I began to cry.

"Misty, I'm sorry." He snapped on the ceiling light. "I'll have them restrung." He took a flashlight from the glove compartment, then opened the car door, and began to look for the pearls. I wrapped the ones I still held in my hand in a tissue, then opened my door and started to get out.

"You'd better stay in the car," he said in a tired voice. "Some of the pearls are probably in your clothing." He got in and handed a few of the beads to me, then started the engine.

We were almost home when he broke the silence. "I can't ever seem to get along with women," he said. He seemed to be talking more to himself than to me. "I thought you were an experienced woman—that you'd like some attention." He took out his cigarette case. "Wrong again."

At my parents' home he walked me to the door. I was grateful Mother wasn't waiting up. "I'll look in the car in the morning for the pearls. Then I'll come by and get the ones you have and have them fixed." He didn't offer to kiss me goodnight, and I was relieved.

I was also relieved the next morning when Mother told me Dad had gone in early to have breakfast with a client. It was bad enough to have to tell her all about Paul and the pearls, without having Dad threatening to do something drastic! I put the broken necklace on the kitchen table. "So, Mother, I don't know if he'll come by this morning while

I'm at Bible School, or later on in the day." I picked up my purse and lesson book and kissed her goodbye.

When I saw Melissa drive into the church lot, I walked over to help her with Mark. Denise jumped out of the car and ran over to greet some other little girls. Melissa handed me a diaper bag, then lifted Mark out of the car seat. "Well? Did you enjoy your date with Paul?" I hesitated, and knew she could probably read the answer on my face. I wasn't good at hiding my feelings.

"He is sort of a braggart," she said. "We all know it, but down deep, he's really a nice guy."

"I'm sure he is—down deep," I said.

"Are you going to date him again?"

"Probably not." I flipped my hair back over my shoulders. "For one thing, I doubt if he'll ever ask me." As we walked toward the church door, I told her how angry I'd been about the pearls, but I didn't tell her exactly how they'd gotten broken. After all, as Glenn said, you can't blame a man for acting like a man. But how did I always manage to get myself into these situations? Was it my fault? Were all men like that? Glenn wasn't. But of course he was different because he was a man of God.

"If you're not going to date him again, I'll tell you some things," Melissa said, grinning like a pixie. "Last night when he said he was in Transportation, Mark and I just about died! Know what he does for a living? He sells cars!" She laughed and clapped her hands together. "I guess he *is* in transportation!"

I smiled. "Why would he want to deceive me?"

"To play the big shot. He doesn't own that Cadillac—it's a dealers' car! I told you he wanted to impress you. He claims he doesn't want to get married, but I think he does."

"Well, he's certainly going about it the wrong way," I said, remembering the struggle in the front seat.

"And when he said he wanted to take you out in his boat, I almost choked!"

"Doesn't he own a boat, either?"

"Sure, he owns a boat—a rowboat!"

We both laughed, then I became serious. "Poor guy. He must be a pathological liar."

Melissa shrugged. "I don't know if he's that bad—but he's definitely a blowhard. In spite of that, I like him. He's bought Markie a lot of things. I'm sure he'd like to have a baby of his own."

The church bus rolled into the lot and stopped. I couldn't be sure, but it looked just like the bus I used to ride when I was little. When the folding door slammed back, children spewed forth like a warm bottle of pop.

"Speaking of babies," I said, "you'd better get Markie into the nursery. You've got to help get all these kids rounded up and in line for the rehearsal."

"We've been at this all morning," I said to the director at noon, "and I still can't promise you my kids will say their verses."

She covered her eyes and moaned. "I'm sure PSA has some afternoon flights to Tahiti." Then she looked at me and smiled. "Don't worry, Misty. Our church prayer warriors have prayed for this Vacation Bible School for a long time. It's God's program. He'll handle it."

I said goodbye to Melissa, then hurried home. With all my heart I hoped Paul had come and gone.

When I turned onto our street, I drew in my breath. A silver car was parked in front of our house. As I got closer my heart began to pound like a drum. It was Glenn's Honda! I parked and forced myself to pick up my bag and the lesson materials—calmly. With deliberation, I closed the car door, locked it, drew a deep breath, and walked sedately toward the porch.

CHAPTER 19

By the time I opened the front door, I was so breathless I was afraid I wouldn't be able to speak. How dear he was! Of all the men I'd known in the past, Glenn was by far the best. He was the only one who had never tried to make advances, and yet, we were able to talk about everything —including sex. I remembered how he had taken care of me when I was sick. I knew in my heart he still loved me. Although it hurt for him to believe I was a thief, as well as a promiscuous woman—even that was understandable. Men had been executed for less evidence than there had been against me.

I rushed in the door, ready to speak his name, but the person who got up from Dad's chair and came toward me was Candy. I looked around to see if Glenn were there, too, but the only other person in the room was Mother.

That was a disappointment, but it was great to see my friend. "Candy!" We hugged each other. "How did you find me?"

"Don't you remember giving me your address?"

"Oh, yes! And I'm so glad I did!" Mother was standing by, smiling. "Have you met my mother?"

"Oh, sure." She gave me a sidelong glance. "She's already given me milk and cookies."

"How long can you stay? Stay all night! You can go with me tonight—"

"Can't. I promised Glenn I'd turn around and go right back up the mountain."

"Oh, foo. How come you're driving Glenn's car?"

"It beats my thumb, for one thing. But he's the reason I'm here. He would have come himself, but he's buried in things he's got to do."

"What's happening? Here, sit down." I pulled her down beside me on the couch and Mother sat down in her chair.

"First—I'm to deliver this." She pulled a letter from her big canvas shoulder bag and handed it to me. It was on Royce Inn stationery. I read aloud so Mother could hear, too.

Dear Misty,

Excuse this scrawling, but I'm trying to get this done so Candy can leave. I had planned to come myself, but we had a crisis here last night. The shower in Fourteen flooded everything, including the front lobby. Workmen and plumbers are everywhere. We closed the dining room for the day, and I am sending Candy as my diplomat to give you my deepest, most humble apology for thinking, even for a moment, that you had taken the money. I hope you can forgive me. I would have telephoned but I was afraid you might hang up on me. She'll tell you the rest.

Love,
Glenn

I could barely see Candy through my tears. Exonerated! Suddenly, I couldn't help but burst into sobs. Candy touched my hand. I laced my fingers through hers and

162

squeezed hard. "Okay. I'm all right now. Tell me every-thing."

She took a deep breath. "Everything?"

"Everything!"

"In the first place, I thought Glenn and Dennis were going to have a knock-down-dragout the next morning when Glenn discovered that you were gone. Glenn even grabbed Dennis by the shirt!"

I put my hand over my mouth. "I can't believe it!"

"He said Dennis should have kept you, that you were in no condition to go anywhere."

I shrugged. "He was probably right." I flicked a glance at Mother. "I wasn't making very good decisions that night."

"You know something, Misty? I think Glenn is in love with you!"

I could feel myself glowing inside, but I laughed it off. "Don't be ridiculous."

"No, he is. He's been mopin' around ever since you left. Anyway, the big news is that about a week after you were gone, Irene got loop-legged drunk and came up to my room. She wanted me to help her find Dennis, but I finally talked her out of that. 'You don't need to worry about him,' I told her. 'He's just playing poker somewhere with the boys.' And then she grinned like a witch, and said, 'Yeah, I got rid of the competition.' And I said—"

"I knew it!" I interrupted. "I knew she planted that money!"

"She's one crazy woman. Anyhow, the next day I kept trying to figure out if I should tell Glenn or Dennis, and one part of me said, 'Why bother? Don't get involved. But another part of me thought what a good kid you are, con-siderin' you're white—"

Mother's eyes opened wide, then she looked down in her

lap. I laughed and hugged Candy. "Go ahead," I urged.

"So I told the boss man, and—are you ready?" Her eyes crinkled. "He fired her!" She made the victory sign with her fingers.

"No!" I was ashamed of the pleasure I was feeling. Poor Irene, she really needed counseling, but I felt like shouting. "What about the dining room? Who's doing the cooking?"

"Glenn got Mrs. Bennett to take over the cooking."

"Mary Jo? But what about her own place?"

"She told me she was relieved to have a real job, doing something she enjoyed doing. She wasn't getting enough business to pay her butane bill."

"I can't believe so much could happen so fast!"

"That's only half of it. Jean's back as hostess, and Debbie's a waitress, part-time."

I was thoroughly enjoying all the news, and I watched Candy intently. I suddenly realized how much she meant to me. I had an impulse to hug her, but knew she'd say something caustic if I did. It seemed to me she was lovelier than ever. Today her black hair was piled high on her head, tied with a lamé scarf, which showed off her gold leaf earrings to good advantage. She wore several thin gold bracelets that tinkled with every movement. As I looked at her, I discovered she was also wearing a diamond. I grabbed her hand. "Candy! When—who—?"

She beamed her answer. "I guess that dude learned his lesson."

"I'm so glad for you!" Mother stood up and came over to admire the ring. "When are you going to get married?"

"Before school starts—and guess who's going to marry us?"

I shrugged. "Glenn! That's who!" She raised an eyebrow and glanced up at Mother. "I never went to church much in L.A., so I wouldn't know where to go for a preacher. Anyway, I like the idea of getting married in the mountains, don't you?'' There was a dreamy look in her eyes, then she chuckled. "Besides," she drew herself up with an exaggerated air of superiority, "I think it's appropriate to have the nuptial ceremony performed by the gentleman who gave me the position that caused my fiancé to come to his senses!''

I laughed and slapped at her. Mother looked bewildered, smiled politely, and sat back down.

When we had finished talking about her wedding plans, I asked, "What about Dennis? How does he feel about Irene being gone?''

"I don't know. I think Dennis is mixed up about her." She raised an eyebrow and touched her lip with her tongue. "I saw him hug her a few times. Of course, everybody knew how she felt about him, so maybe he just felt sorry for her. I don't know, though. Both the guys seem pretty testy around each other, and especially since Irene's been gone. But there's so much business at the inn, nobody's got much time to complain.''

"Who's on the switchboard?''

She rolled her eyes. "Not me. I goof that thing up every time I get close to it.''

"Now Candy, that's not so! You did just fine when I was there!''

"Did I? How about that." She looked at me slyly. "But those callers don't leave no tips!''

"You're rotten, Candy! Poor Dennis and Glenn, with no relief, just because you're money-mad.''

"Which brings me to item two on the agenda. Glenn wants you back, and he said he might not be able to match the salary you had in Reno, but he'd do his best.''

I drew in my breath. "He couldn't afford that kind of money for a switchboard operator!''

"Oh, but you wouldn't be on the desk all the time. I think he had something like assistant manager in mind."

My mouth dropped and I looked over at Mother. "But how—"

"Dennis is leaving as soon as you come—if you *will* come. So Glenn won't have to pay his salary or commission."

Mother stood up. "I'm going to put our lunch on the table." She went to the kitchen and left Candy and me to sit in silence.

My mind whirled like the slot machines in Reno. Did I want to go back to work at the Royce Inn? Or should I stay here and continue to look for work? The interview at SOHIO had gone well. They might be calling me. There had been a couple of other promising interviews . . .

"Misty?" Mother called.

"Excuse me, Candy." I went to the kitchen.

"Is she going to stay for lunch?" Mother asked.

"Is it all right?"

"Of course. I just wanted to know how much salad to make." She beckoned for me to come near, then whispered, "That Paul was here."

"Did you give him the pearls?" I whispered back.

She shook her head firmly. "I didn't even invite him in. I told him I would have them fixed myself! So he gave me four pearls and his card, and said for me to send him the bill."

"Well, do it!" I rasped.

In a normal voice, she asked. "Misty, are you going back to that place?"

"I don't know, Mother." I bit my lip and sighed deeply. I wanted to. I wanted to see the mountains. And Glenn. But I didn't want to make any more mistakes.

After lunch I said to Candy, "Can't you stay for the program tonight? My little class is darling."

166

"I'll bet!" Candy said. "But I'd better get going. What shall I tell Glenn?"

I looked at her for a long moment. "Tell Glenn I'm going to pray about it."

That night at the V.B.S. program I could scarcely sit still. I squirmed more than my second-graders, and the program seemed endless. While all the little kids performed, I was in a dream world of my own. I kept thinking about Glenn. I couldn't imagine him almost fighting over me. The only part of the program that stayed in my mind was when the pastor gave the meditation and quoted the verse, "We love, because he first loved us." God loved me! God loved *me*! In a rush I realized he had answered my prayer! He had cleared my name, and if I wanted to accept it, He had provided a good job with a man I respected. Glenn's face appeared in my mind, and I felt a warm glow all through my body.

That night I couldn't go to sleep. My thoughts were about the successful program we had presented and what the director had said about prayer. In the dark, I stretched out my arm and whispered, "Here's my hand, Lord. Please lead me."

As I got closer to Donnerville, I felt my heart beating in my throat. The scenery was so beautiful—deep blue skies, tall pines, clean air. I inhaled deeply. I couldn't wait to get there!

At last I saw the sign, "Donnerville," and I let out a little squeal. When I turned in the driveway of the inn, my hands were sweaty and my stomach was churning. I leaped out of the car and grabbed my purse. I could get the rest of my things later. I ran around the building and raced up the steps. As I crossed the veranda, Glenn stepped out the front door. I stopped short, suddenly embarrassed.

"Misty—you're finally here. Am I glad to see you!" He reached for my hand and pulled me close. I could feel him tremble, and I had a great desire to be in his arms, but he only kissed my cheek and released me. I looked up at him. He seemed taller and bigger than ever. His green eyes were sparkling, and his gleaming teeth even brighter than I remembered. "You look beautiful!"

"It's good to see you, too," I murmured. I looked around at the desk and saw Dennis.

"Hi, Misty," he called, smiling cordially.

Mary Jo, Candy, and a woman I'd never met came out of the dining room, and in spite of several people in the lobby, Mary Jo and Candy hugged and kissed me. Candy said, "Misty, this is Jean. See? She's all over her pneumonia." Jean was petite, even smaller than I. Her short hair was curly, and her gray eyes seemed enormous in a heart-shaped face. She looked thin and pale, but her smile and handshake were strong. Bret and Rick also appeared, smiling and nodding as if they, too, were really glad to see me.

"Why don't you fellows go get Misty's luggage?" Glenn said. He took the car keys out of my hand and handed them to Bret.

I looked up at Glenn and almost said, "I love you," but instead I asked, "Am I staying in Seven?"

Glenn smiled down at me. "Yes. For the time being. But sometime, I'd like to tell you about my plans for your future living quarters." His eyes held mine for a long moment.

In a couple of days, after I'd settled in, it seemed as though I'd never been gone. The weeks sped by and, within a short time, Dennis had taught me the bookkeeping system, where to buy supplies, how to make advance reservations, and a lot of other information that I would have to know if I were to be the help Glenn needed. Things had changed a great deal in the short time I'd been gone. Although Glenn

168

and Dennis still spent time on the desk, another young man, Steve, had been hired to register guests and help with their luggage. He was slender and wiry and didn't talk very much, but he seemed eager to please.

"He's one of the kids from church," Glenn told me one morning at breakfast. We had resumed our habit of eating together in the morning. Instead of Irene's delicious pastry, we ate Mary Jo's fat biscuits, served with her own raspberry jam. "He tried to commit suicide about six months ago," Glenn went on. "He was into drugs, but since he accepted Christ, he seems to be completely recovered."

"Are you working with the high school kids?" I asked.

"I'm working with all of them—junior and senior high. Only about fifteen or twenty kids in the combined age groups come on a regular basis." He finished his coffee. "It's not too good to mix the ages. The older kids are insulted!" He laughed, and ran his fingers through his hair. I had a strong urge to run *my* fingers through his hair. "We need another leader . . ." He lifted his hands helplessly. "Same old story—not enough help."

"*I'd* like to help—if you want me."

His eyes widened. "If I want—!"

I told him about V.B.S. and how much I'd enjoyed it. "But I was working with second-graders. I don't know much about older kids." I grinned at him. "I was an only child, you know."

We were silent a moment, looking into each other's eyes. I felt his hand on mine. "I didn't know you were an only child, Misty. But I do know you're the only woman for me."

I closed my eyes. My head seemed to spin and I lost my breath. I turned my hand under his, and gripped his fingers. When I opened my eyes, his face was near mine. He took both my hands and pulled me to him, and for the first time, he kissed me as a man kisses a woman. I felt a bolt of hot lightning inside, warming even my fingertips. I wanted the kiss to go on forever, and I pressed as close to him as I could. When he pulled away, we were both flushed and breathless. His green eyes seemed to have firelights in them. In a husky whisper, he said, "Misty, my love, my treasure! Will you marry me?"

Although I've tried, I can't remember my answer. Did I say, "Oh yes!" or "Oh, Glenn!" or "Oh, darling!" Maybe I only kissed him, but whatever, there was no question about my answer.

I couldn't wait to tell Candy. Every chance we got, we talked about love and marriage.

One day Glenn asked me if I would rather have his mother's engagement ring or a new one. Deep inside, I really wished I could have a new diamond in a modern setting. I had never seen his mother's ring, but I assumed it was an average stone in an old-fashioned basket design. But, since we were struggling to make a success of the inn, and especially as we looked forward to the time it could become a Christian Conference Center, I felt it would be wise to accept his mother's ring.

"I'm glad," he said. "It has great sentimental value, at least to me. Come back to the apartment and I'll get it." When he showed it to me, my face got hot and I couldn't speak. It was a yellow gold solitaire, with a magnificient diamond.

"It's a full karat," Glenn said. "Dad bought it for Mom just a few months before she died." He put it on my finger, and pulled me close. We kissed until we were both trembling. He cleared his throat and pushed me away. "Let's get out of here," he said. I laughed and held my hand up so we both could see the flashing gem.

"I can't believe it fits exactly!" For the first few days I

couldn't take my eyes off it for more than a few minutes at a time, and at night I often put it to my lips and drifted off to sleep to dream that I was kissing Glenn.

One day I tried to tell Candy how I felt. "I know I loved Dave. I wanted to be with him all the time. But maybe it was just for security—to have a boyfriend. I really didn't enjoy his kisses."

"Well, darlin'," Candy drawled, "take it from a pro. You weren't in love with that dude."

"I *thought* I was. And then I thought I was infatuated with Dennis." I felt my cheeks burning.

"Ah, ha! I thought there was some hanky-panky goin' on!"

I stamped my foot. "No, there wasn't!" I grinned. "But I have to admit, I felt more excited around him than Dave."

"Oh, he has charisma, all right!"

"But never have I experienced the depth of feeling I have for Glenn." I closed my eyes and sighed. "I wish the whole world could be in love like I am."

There wasn't too much time to think about love, however. Even though the tourist season was almost over, thanks to Dennis's efforts, we had reservations well into the winter months. Every day was full, with people coming and going, problems to solve, ruffled feathers to smooth. Dennis was the kindest and most patient of teachers. Although he would soon be leaving, he did his best to anticipate any problems we might have.

"What are you going to do when you leave here, Dennis?" I asked one afternoon during a lull.

"I'm going back to Reno—or maybe Vegas. I've been making some connections."

"It's too quiet for you here, isn't it?"

He smiled and shrugged. "I guess it is—and yet, I'd give

a lot to have the peace old Glenn has." I wanted to tell him about *my* newfound peace, but it wasn't easy to put into words. I had tried to tell Candy how I put my hand in God's, but she hadn't seemed to understand, and quickly changed the subject.

Candy got married in the little Community Church the first Saturday night in September. Her whole family was there for the wedding, and I felt honored that she had invited me to be a bridesmaid. As she said her vows, I repeated them to myself. I longed to be Mrs. Glenn Royce.

In October, Dennis packed up and left. We gave him a fantastic going-away party. Mary Jo outdid herself, and we invited many of the townspeople who were close friends of the family. Once, when Dennis and I happened to be at the punch bowl, he said, "Misty, you are a very special person. Glenn's a lucky man. I wish I could be more like him." His sincerity brought tears to my eyes and, at that moment, I felt a brotherly love for him. But it was a relief for him to be gone. I could never be with him without remembering my indiscretion. Also, I was anxious to take over my duties without his watching over my shoulder. Debbie told us that she and her aunt had seen him with Irene while they were on a shopping spree in Reno.

"He'll marry her someday," Glenn predicted.

Glenn and I planned to get married just before Christmas. Mother and Dad wanted us to come home and get married in the church in Stockton, and we considered it. But I felt as Candy had, that I wanted to say my vows in the splendor and serenity of the mountains. In Glenn's little church.

Candy and her new husband were coming up for the wedding, and she and Debbie, as bridesmaids, were going to wear deep red velvet dresses. My gown was white velvet and lace and I would wear a short veil.

The afternoon before we got married, Glenn and I decorated the little church with pine boughs and wide red, satin bows. Once, when he had his arms around me, he said. "When did you fall in love with me?"

I laughed and shook my head. "I don't know. I remember when I first met you I thought you were very nice, but 'not my type!' Isn't that awful?"

He kissed my hair. "Did you know I prayed that you would learn to love me?"

I gazed at him in wonder. "Did you really? Oh, Glenn, God certainly answered your prayer, because I do love you—so much!" I buried my face in his chest. Then I looked up at him. "Glenn! I just thought of something! In Vacation Bible School the pastor used the verse, "We love, because He first loved us!"

Glenn nodded. "That's right. He did love us first. When we discover that, then He becomes irresistible and it's easier for us to love Him."

"That's exactly how it is with you and me, too," I whispered. "I love *you*, because you first loved *me*!"

He took me in his arms, and I closed my eyes. His lips covered mine, warm, demanding, and my arms went up and around his neck. No one in all the world could be as happy as I! I thought of the night I had run away from Reno. I had found more than a refuge from heartbreak the night I walked into the hotel. Love had walked in beside me.

MEET THE AUTHOR

MAB GRAFF HOOVER is a romantic person who loves writing romance novels. Born in Parsons, Kansas, Mab now lives in Bellflower, California, with her much-adored husband. She is a homemaker, mother of two children, grandmother, and a full-time writer.

Mab has written several inspirational books for Zondervan, including *God Loves My Kitchen Best,* and *God Even Likes My Pantry.* On writing, she says, "It's good to dwell on happy and light thoughts." Although Mab's in the later years of her life, she is devoted to celebrating the goodness of life with love, old-fashioned romance, and roses, "red ones, with lots of baby's breath and fern."

Serenade Books are inspirational romances in contemporary settings, designed to bring you a joyful, heart-lifting reading experience.

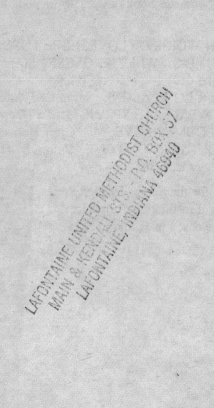